I Want My Mummy

Bethany House Books by
Bill Myers

Bloodhounds, Inc.
CHILDREN'S MYSTERY SERIES

The Ghost of KRZY
The Mystery of the Invisible Knight
Phantom of the Haunted Church
Invasion of the UFOs
Fangs for the Memories
The Case of the Missing Minds
The Secret of the Ghostly Hot Rod
I Want My Mummy
The Curse of the Horrible Hair Day
The Scam of the Screwball Wizards

Nonfiction

The Dark Side of the Supernatural
Hot Topics, Tough Questions

Bill Myers' Web site: *www.BillMyers.com*

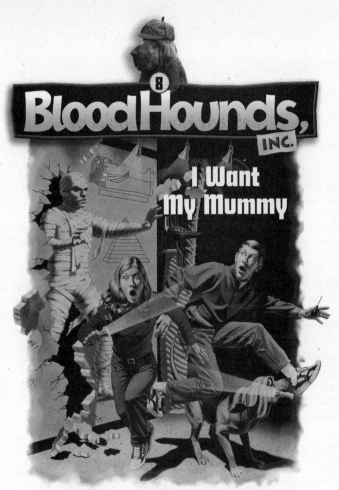

BloodHounds, INC.

8

I Want My Mummy

Bill Myers

with DAVE WIMBISH

x

BETHANY HOUSE PUBLISHERS
MINNEAPOLIS, MINNESOTA 55438

Published by Bethany House Publishers
A Ministry of Bethany Fellowship International
11400 Hampshire Avenue South
Minneapolis, Minnesota 55438
www.bethanyhouse.com

Printed in the United States of America by
Bethany Press International, Minneapolis, Minnesota 55438

Library of Congress Cataloging-in-Publication Data

Myers, Bill, 1953–
   I want my mummy / by Bill Myers.
      p. cm. — (Bloodhounds, Inc., ; 8)
Summary: Panic grips Midvale when a mummy disappears from an Egyptian
exhibit at the museum, leaving it up to Sean and Melissa to solve the mystery.
   ISBN 1–55661–492–6 (pbk.)
   [1. Mummies—Fiction. 2. Christian life—Fiction. 3. Mystery and detective
stories.] I. Title.
   PZ7.M98234 Iaf 2000
   [Fic]—dc21

                                                  00–010527

To Steve, Shelley, and Adam . . .

Thanks for all the years of inspiration!

BILL MYERS is a youth worker, creative writer, and film director who co-created the "McGee and Me!" book and video series; his work has received over forty national and international awards. His many youth books include THE INCREDIBLE WORLDS OF WALLY MCDOOGLE series, his teen books: *Hot Topic, Tough Questions, Faith Encounter,* and *Forbidden Doors,* as well as his adult trilogy: *Blood of Heaven, Threshold,* and *Fire of Heaven.*

Contents

1. The Case Begins.................................... 9
2. Has Anybody Seen My Mummy? 25
3. What's the Matter, Cat Got Your Voice Chip?..... 43
4. Mrs. Tubbs: Street-Fighter........................ 57
5. A Cemetery Stroll 69
6. A Mummy Makeover 79
7. Strangerer and Strangerer 85
8. Mummy Mia, Is That You, Mrs. Tubbs? 97
9. Where There's Smoke 105
10. Wrapping Up....................................115

*There is neither Jew nor Greek,
slave nor free, male nor female,
for you are all one in Christ Jesus.*

Galatians 3:28, NIV

1

The Case Begins

TUESDAY, 20:07 PDST

BEEP ... BEEP ... BEEP ... BEEP ...

The big truck's warning horn echoed through the night as Tom, the old, balding driver, slowly backed his vehicle up the steep hill toward the loading dock of the Midvale Museum.

Standing on the loading dock, Tom's partner, Harry (who was about half as old and half as bald), motioned for the truck to keep coming. "No problem," he shouted. "Plenty of room."

Harry looked up at the full moon. Even though it was a warm fall evening, he felt a shiver run across his shoulders. Most of the time he loved working for the museum, but sometimes it gave him the creeps. He had what some people called an "overactive imagination." And there were so many weird old statues and things here, that every once in a while he had nightmares about them coming to life and chasing him.

Harry was a big man—six four, with bulging muscles. He looked like the kind of guy who wouldn't be afraid of anything.

But he was.

Especially this evening. Why, oh why, had he stayed up so late last night watching that *X Files* marathon on TV? He held out his hand, motioning for his partner to stop.

SSSSSSSSSSH . . .

The truck's brakes hissed as it came to a halt several feet from the loading dock.

"Perfect!" Harry shouted.

Tom climbed out of the truck and headed up the steep incline to give his partner a hand.

"So whadd'ya got tonight?" Harry asked.

Tom shrugged. "Not sure. A big crate of some kind. Came all the way from Cairo, Egypt." He unlocked the truck's trailer compartment, swung the doors open wide, and he and Harry stepped inside.

There in the darkness sat a huge wooden crate. Dirty. Dusty.

Harry swallowed hard as he wondered what was inside.

"Come on," Tom said. "Let's get this thing unloaded so we can get out of here."

Harry walked toward the crate, then suddenly stopped in his tracks. "Did you hear that?" he whispered.

"Hear what?"

"I don't know." Harry pointed at the crate. "I think something's moving in there."

Tom shook his head. "I didn't hear anything. It was probably just the wind."

"There's no wind tonight," Harry said.

"Well, then, maybe you heard a dog or a cat or something," Tom said. "But you did not hear anything moving inside this box. Now, get over here and give me a hand!"

Harry didn't want Tom to think he was a chicken, so he grabbed an end of the crate and helped lift it down to the street.

Tom grunted. "This thing is heavy!"

"And the steep driveway doesn't help much," Harry complained as they started toward the loading dock. Unfortunately, they'd only taken a step or two before . . .

"AUGH . . ."

Harry let out a bloodcurdling scream and . . .

K-THUMP!

. . . dropped his end of the crate.

"What's wrong?!" Tom cried.

"Don't you hear it?" Harry shouted, pointing down at

the crate. "Whatever's in that thing is alive!"

"I don't hear anything!"

"Well, I do," Harry said, starting to back away. "What if it's—I don't know—a monster or something."

"A monster?!" Tom shook his head. "You've been watching too many scary videos again! A monster in a big crate?" He let out a short laugh. "That kind of stuff only takes place in Hollywood. Nothing like that ever happens in—"

EEEEEEEEEE!

Tom came to a stop. He wasn't sure if that was a screech owl looking for supper, the squeaky brakes of the nearby garbage truck making its rounds, or maybe, just maybe, something screaming inside the crate!

Whatever it was, he suddenly . . .

K-RASH!

. . . let go of his end of the crate and took off running.

"Outta my way!" he shouted.

"No! You get out of my way!" Harry shouted as they both sprinted into the darkness for their lives.

Unfortunately, the crate was so heavy and the driveway was so steep that the crate immediately started to . . .

SCRAPE . . . SLIP, SCRAPE . . . SCRAPE . . .

. . . slide down the driveway. Faster and faster it went. And then faster still until finally . . .

KER-THUNK!

. . . it slammed into a curb at the bottom of the hill near the trash dumpsters.

Meanwhile, Tom and Harry were coming very close to setting a world speed record as they continued running from the truck. At least for a while. But pretty soon, Tom's common sense got the better of him, and he shouted, "Harry, slow down. Harry, hold up a minute." He reached out to Harry's shoulder and pulled him to a stop.

"What are you doing?" Harry gasped, trying to catch his breath.

"We've got to go back," Tom said.

"Back!" Harry wheezed. "Are you nuts?"

"Come on, Harry. There's no such things as monsters—you know that," Tom said. "Our imaginations just got the better of us."

"But—"

"Come on."

"But . . . but . . ."

Tom shrugged. "Well, I'm going back." With that, he turned and started toward the museum. "Come on," he shouted over his shoulder. "Let's get that thing unloaded and call it a night."

"Tom!" Harry shouted.

13

But Tom wasn't stopping.

"TOM!"

He still wasn't stopping.

"Okay . . . okay," Harry finally whined. "Wait for me!" He didn't really want to go back to the museum, but he didn't want to be by himself in the dark, either. Reluctantly, he followed his partner back toward the museum.

Suddenly they both stopped dead in their tracks.

"Look!" Tom shouted, pointing toward the spot where the crate had landed in the driveway. "It's . . . GONE!"

"I see that!" Harry cried. "What are we gonna do? What are we gonna do?"

"I don't know!" Tom shouted. "I don't know!"

TUESDAY, 20: 11 PDST

The cookout on Sean and Melissa Hunter's patio was in full swing. Their dad was hosting it in honor of their new neighbor, Abdul Azziz, who had recently come to Midvale from Cairo, Egypt. Lots of folks were there— Mayor Jenkins, a couple of city councilmen, and some representatives from Midvale's small Arab community, including Abdul's brother-in-law, Hakeem Haddad, the new curator of the museum.

Oh yes, and there was one other person—Mrs. Tubbs, the kids' snooty next-door neighbor. At the moment, she was trying just a little too hard to impress the handsome Abdul.

"Me happy . . . you here," she said. "Me happy . . . you come America. Welcome!"

Sean and Melissa could only roll their eyes, trying not to laugh as the woman pointed to Abdul's hot dog.

"Me hope you likee doggie doggie," Mrs. Tubbs said.

Abdul smiled, but it was a frightened kind of smile. And when Mrs. Tubbs finally moved away, Abdul turned to Melissa, whispering, "What in the world is wrong with that woman? Is she. . . ?" He pointed at the side of his head and made little circular motions with his finger.

Melissa nodded and giggled. "Yes, but just a little."

"Excuse me, Abdul?" It was Sean and Melissa's dad. "I want you to meet a friend of mine. Herbie here is the chief engineer at my radio station." (What Dad didn't say was that Herbie was also the *only* engineer at radio station KRZY. Nor did he mention that he was somewhat "accident prone.")

"Very pleased to meet you," Herbie said, trying his best to make a good impression as he stuck out his hand to shake. He would have made a better impression if he had remembered to set down his hot dog first.

SQUISH . . .

15

"Oh, sorry," Herbie said as he realized he'd just squashed the hot dog all over Abdul's hand—a hot dog with more than its fair share of mustard, relish, and lots of dripping ketchup. "Here, let me get a napkin and clean that up."

Abdul gave another frightened smile to Melissa as Herbie reached for a napkin and went to work on the man's hand.

But Dad, who was used to Herbie's antics, continued without missing a beat. "Abdul will be staying in Midvale for a few months because he's in charge of an important exhibit that's going on display at the Midvale Museum."

"You don't say!" Herbie said. By now he'd dropped to his knees and was wiping the ketchup off of Abdul's shoes. "What exhibit is that?"

"I'm traveling with the mummy of King Tut-Tut the Thirty-Third," Abdul answered. "As you know, my brother-in-law is the new curator of the Midvale Museum, and he arranged for me to come here. He nodded toward Hakeem Haddad, who sat quietly on the other side of the yard, talking with a couple of friends.

"Really?" Herbie said as he rose and tossed the napkins away. "Wow!" He sounded impressed, even though he probably had no idea who King Tut-Tut the Thirty-Third was. (For that matter, he probably didn't know anything about Kings Tut-Tut the First through the Thirty-Second, either.)

"That's right," Dad said. "And, of course, I want to do a big story on it for KRZY News."

"Of course," Herbie agreed.

"In the meantime, I thought it would be nice to invite Abdul over for a cookout so he could meet some of the neighbors."

Suddenly Mrs. Tubbs stepped back between them, doing her best job of flirting. "Oh, Abdul," she gushed, "I didn't know you speak English so well! You must have learned awfully quick!"

"Well, you see, I attended Harvard University, and I—"

"That's just marvelous," she interrupted. "Say, I was wondering, how's the pharaoh these days?"

Abdul looked puzzled. "Egypt hasn't had a pharaoh in at least three thousand ye—"

But Mrs. Tubbs was too busy trying to impress him to listen. "I'm glad to hear he's doing well," she interrupted again. "And are your people working on any new pyramids or anything?"

The expression on Abdul's face clearly said, "Will somebody please rescue me from this woman?"

And Melissa knew just how to do it. She tapped Mrs. Tubbs on the shoulder. "Excuse me," she said, "but I think there's one more hamburger on the grill."

"Really?" Mrs. Tubbs batted her eyes in Abdul's direction. "I'll be right back," she said, then rushed to nab that hamburger before someone else beat her to it.

"Thank you, young lady," Abdul whispered to Melissa. "Thank you very much."

Melissa's dad put his arm around her. "This is my daughter, Melissa," he said. "We call her Misty."

"It's a pleasure to meet you, Misty," Abdul smiled.

"Did I hear my dad say that you came here with the mummy of King Tut-Tut the Thirty-Third?" Melissa asked.

"Yes."

"Wow! Wasn't he the richest and most powerful of all the ancient pharaohs?"

"That's right." Abdul smiled. "I see you know your history."

"EEAAAGHHH!"

Suddenly someone screamed.

"Look out!" Mayor Jenkins cried.

"What is it?" Dad shouted.

"Bats! Hundreds of them!"

Everyone followed his pointing finger to see an army of flying bats swooping in from the northwest, beating their wings furiously against the night sky. There were so many that they briefly blocked the light of the moon.

"EAGGHHH!" Mrs. Tubbs screamed. "They're coming to drink my blood!" (The woman was definitely

18

overreacting. But considering what she'd been through during *Fangs for the Memories,* who could blame her?)

Though they were dozens of feet overhead, she waved her hands at the bats, trying to keep them away. Unfortunately, those were the same hands she was using to hold her hamburger.

The same hamburger that flew off of the plate and . . .

SMACK!

. . . clobbered Mayor Jenkins on the side of the head.

Mustard dripped down his face. Tomatoes fell onto his shirt. And, thinking it was also part of a bat attack, he frantically waved his own arms, causing his open can of Diet Pepsi to . . .

SPTTTTTTT!

. . . spray all over Mrs. Tubbs' face, which caused her to scream even louder.

"I'm bleeding! I'm bleeding!" she cried. "I've been bit by a bat, and I'm bleeding!"

Looking for some weapon to defend herself, she grabbed the long-handled fork Dad had been using to grill the hot dogs. She flung it toward the attacking bats with all her might.

WHOOOOOOSH!

The fork zipped through the air faster than a Randy Johnson fastball.

Unfortunately, her aim wasn't as good. Instead of hitting a bat, the fork skimmed the top of Herbie's head, catching his new toupee and knocking it to the ground.

Well, not exactly "to the ground." Instead, it landed on top of Mrs. Tubbs' spoiled cat, Precious.

"Meowrrr! Hisssss!"

Naturally, the big cat wasn't crazy about this, and he tried to scramble for safety. Then, of course, there was Melissa and Sean's bloodhound, Slobs.

"AROOO!"

Normally, Slobs liked nothing better than chasing that fat cat, but not now. Instead, she took one look at the thing on Precious's head, thought it was some sort of hairy monster, and took off in the opposite direction.

"AROOO! AROOO! AROO!"

"My hair! My hair! Bring back my hair!" Herbie scrambled after the cat but slipped on one of the mayor's tomatoes and went sprawling to the ground.

The next few minutes were anything but calm.

Precious yowled and spit, trying to get free of the "monster" on his head.

Slobs howled and barked.

Herbie kept chasing his runaway wig, shouting, "My hair, my hair, my hair!"

And Mrs. Tubbs kept screaming, "They want to drink my blood! They want to drink my blood!" Of course, by now the bats were gone, but that didn't stop Mrs. Tubbs.

Finally, Melissa got her attention. "Look, Mrs. Tubbs. Look, they're gone. They're all gone."

The woman stopped and looked up into the sky.

"See," Melissa said. "All gone. Besides, I think they were just fruit bats."

"Don't lie to me!" Mrs. Tubbs snapped. "I know a vampire bat when I see one."

"But, Mrs. Tubbs . . ."

"I'm afraid I must be leaving," she said, fluttering her eyes in Abdul's direction. "I must lie down. I'm a delicate woman, you know, and I cannot take this sort of excitement."

She turned on her heels . . .

"WHOAAAAA!"

. . . slipped on the mayor's smashed tomato, and . . .

KERWHACK!

. . . tumbled face first to the ground!

"Are you okay, Mrs. Tubbs?" Sean asked as he grabbed her elbow, helping her to her feet.

"Ow! Ow! Ow!" She clasped her hand to her jaw. "I tink I broke my toot!"

"You what?" Melissa asked as she took hold of the woman's other elbow.

"My toot! My toot!" Mrs. Tubbs screamed.

One of the Arab businessmen rushed over. "I think she broke her tooth. Is that what you're saying, ma'am?"

Mrs. Tubbs nodded. "It hurt!" she moaned.

"I'm sure it does," the man said. "But you are in luck because I'm a dentist. We can go to my office right now, and I'll get you all patched up."

Fear showed in Mrs. Tubbs' eyes. She didn't know anything about this man. He wasn't even an American! What if he didn't know what he was doing? She wasn't sure she could trust him. But that tooth hurt so badly.

"I'll go along with you, if that will make you feel better," Abdul offered.

"Okay! Okay! Tank you!" She gratefully took his arm and they headed off.

As he watched them leave, Dad shook his head.

"Pretty weird," Herbie agreed as he stood beside him. "But Mrs. Tubbs is definitely an unusual woman."

"I wasn't thinking about Mrs. Tubbs," Dad said. "I was thinking about all those bats."

The mayor, who had finally recovered, joined them and nodded. "You know, I've heard that some Indian tribes believe a swarm of bats is a sign that something bad is going to happen."

Herbie nodded. "I've heard that, too."

"I'm not so sure I believe that," Dad said.

"Then, what caused it?" the mayor asked.

"I don't know." Dad shrugged. "It's been awfully dry around here lately. Maybe the bats were just looking for water."

The mayor looked up at the sky and sighed. "I sure hope you're right."

2

Has Anybody Seen My Mummy?

WEDNESDAY, 7:45 PDST

"Do you mind if I sit with you?"

"Huh?" Melissa opened her eyes to see Spalding standing in the aisle of the bus. She must have dozed off. Last night's barbecue went on longer than it should have, and she had to get up early for today's honor-society field trip. But why on earth would Spalding ask to sit with her? Truth be told, they weren't that crazy about each other. But, truth also be told, she didn't want to be rude.

"Oh, uh, hi." She nodded, then scooted over so he could have a seat. "Sure."

Spalding may not have been the smartest kid at Midvale Middle School, but he thought he was. And he was certainly the richest. Generally, he hung out with his two closest friends—KC, who was the toughest girl in

Midvale, and Bear, who was as big as he was slow.

Melissa and Sean didn't exactly consider Spalding, KC, and Bear to be friends. But they weren't exactly enemies, either. They were just kind of . . . well . . . annoying.

But Dad had always told them that it was important to be nice to others. Ever since they were kids, he'd drilled into them how important it was to live by God's Golden Rule and to treat others as you wanted to be treated yourself. That's why Melissa didn't object when Spalding sat down next to her.

The two of them were among forty of Midvale Middle School's top students who had been invited on this special field trip to the city's museum.

Before Spalding sat down, he took out a handkerchief and carefully wiped off the school-bus seat. "Can't be too careful, you know," he said as he bent down, inspected the seat, and gave it another wipe just to be certain.

Melissa practically sprained her eyes rolling them. "Ahem," she cleared her throat to keep from laughing. "So where are KC and Bear?" she asked.

"Oh, come on," Spalding sniffed. "They may be my friends, but they're hardly honor students." He paused for a moment, then asked, "And your brother?"

"You don't exactly make the honor roll with a D-minus average," she smiled.

Spalding sighed and checked his watch. "Actually, I

hate these honor-student field trips. Who knows what exciting things I'll be missing in my algebra class."

Melissa could only stare at him. He was even stranger than she thought. Still, she tried to be polite. "Aren't you excited about seeing the mummy?" she asked.

"King Tut-Tut the Thirty-Third. Of course I am. Why, did you know that he was born in Alexandria, Egypt, 1,790 years before Christ, that he had 437 rooms in his palace, and that . . ."

Melissa did her best to look interested as Spalding droned on and on. And then on some more.

". . . and that's when he launched a war against the tribes in the southern deserts, and . . ." Spalding continued to babble.

Melissa tried her best to fight off her sleepiness, but it was no use. She could see Spalding's mouth moving, but his words began to fade. What was that he was saying? "Bubble, hubble, fazeez what?" Why wasn't he making sense?

Her eyes were so, so heavy. Maybe if she just closed them. Only for a moment.

"Hubble, fazeez, bubble . . ."

Before she knew it, her head had dropped to her chest, and she began to softly snore.

SNXXX . . .

27

Spalding looked shocked. And then hurt.

But not in Melissa's dream. In her dream, Spalding had come to school with a terrible case of laryngitis. He couldn't even talk. And as she slept, a huge smile spread across her face.

"Humph!" Spalding snorted. He sat back in his seat, folded his arms across his chest, and gave his best spoiled-rich-kid pout . . . all the way to the museum.

WEDNESDAY, 8:05 PDST

Mr. Hakeem Haddad waited anxiously for the kids as they piled off the bus and made their way into the lobby of his museum.

"Welcome to the Midvale Museum!" he said, flashing a smile that would have been right at home in a toothpaste commercial. "We're honored to have you here as we celebrate the unveiling of one of the most important exhibits in our museum's history."

He waited a moment, as if expecting the kids to break into a round of applause.

They didn't. There was only silence.

"Ahem!" He cleared his throat. "Well, if you'll follow me, you are in for a thrill."

The students and teachers followed Mr. Haddad down the hall until they came to a room decorated with palm trees, camels, and pyramids painted upon the walls. In the middle of the room sat something that looked like a giant coffin.

Melissa's heart beat faster as she thought about what was inside: the three-thousand-year-old mummy of King Tut-Tut the Thirty-Third! She'd read so much about this powerful king from the greatest days in the history of Egypt, and now she was actually going to be face-to-face with him. Er, better make that face-to-bandage.

"This," said Mr. Haddad, flashing that blinding smile and gesturing toward the coffin, "is the sarcophagus of the great king who ruled Egypt for more than thirty-five years. And, my friends, you are the first citizens of Midvale to see what lies inside."

He stepped to the sarcophagus and, with a grand flourish, opened the lid wide.

But instead of gasps of excitement from the crowd, there was only silence and shock.

Mr. Haddad smiled at their puzzled faces. "Isn't it amazing?" he asked. "All the majesty! All the glory!"

"All the nothingness!" said Spalding.

"Nothingness? What do you mean?"

"He's right, Mr. Haddad," Melissa said. "There's nothing in there."

29

"Nothing . . . why, that's impossible." The curator turned and looked into the sarcophagus for the first time. He let out a gasp of horror, then crumpled to the floor in a faint.

Melissa was right. It was completely empty.

WEDNESDAY, 8:15 PDST

Mrs. Tubbs sat straight up in bed.

"Who said that?" she cried. She looked around her bedroom, half expecting to see someone standing in the shadows. Nothing. Just Precious curled up at the foot of her bed, snoring in his sleep.

"I must have been dreaming," she said out loud. Sure, that was it. She'd been having a crazy dream because of that bat attack last night. That and the late-night emergency trip to the dentist's office.

Wait a minute!

There it was again!

A man's voice. And it seemed to be coming from . . . somewhere inside her head!

What was that he said?

"Just do it?"

Just do what? She clapped her hands over her ears. But

the voice inside her head only got louder.

WEDNESDAY, 14:50 PDST

"You're kidding me, right?"

Melissa rolled her eyes at her brother. "For the last time, I am not kidding. When Mr. Haddad opened the sarcophagus, it was empty." She fought back the urge to add, "Just like your head."

Melissa and Sean headed home from school along Fourth Street as she tried to tell him what had happened earlier at the museum. But he just didn't get it.

"Well, if the mummy wasn't in its sarfologus . . ."

"Sarcophagus," she corrected him.

"Whatever. If it wasn't there, where is it?"

"How would I know where it is?" she said.

"I mean, do you suppose it's wandering around out there somewhere like in one of those old movies . . . a creature of the night?" He pulled his shirt collar up over his ears, stuck his arms out in front of him, and began walking stiff-legged down the street.

Melissa quit walking and put her hands on her hips. "Would you please stop that! You look stupid enough in those baggy pants of yours."

Sean looked hurt. "What's wrong with my pants?"

"Nothing—if you like wearing pants three sizes too big."

"Well, I think I look cool in them."

"You'll really look cool if they fall off you. They're so big, I'm surprised you can even keep them on."

"Hey, they happen to be the in thing right now."

"Well, if you want to look like a fool, that's up to you," Melissa said. "Now, will you listen to what I'm trying to tell you?"

Sean stomped monster-style back in her direction. "Speak, Master. I will do your bidding."

"Listen," she demanded, "this could be another case for Bloodhounds, Inc., so I'd appreciate it if—"

"Another case?" Sean dropped his arms to his side. "Why didn't you say so?"

"I've been trying. If you'd just stop clowning around and listen."

"So tell me," he insisted.

"Well, after Mr. Haddad was revived, I gave him our business card. I told him Bloodhounds, Inc. would be happy to try to find his mummy for him."

"And. . . ?"

"And he said he'd pay us a thousand dollars if we could find the mummy and bring it back in good shape."

"A thousand dollars!" Sean practically choked. "Did

you say a thousand . . . *dollars*?"

Melissa nodded.

"Just think what I could do with that money!"

"Now, don't get carried away," she warned. "We've got to find the mummy before we get the money."

"Mummy?" An electronic-sounding voice came from Sean's digital watch. "Did I hear someone say, 'mummy'?"

"Oh, hi, Jeremiah," Sean said, glancing at his watch. A tiny green-skinned, red-haired, leprechaun-like figure was looking back at him. The little guy was pulsating with electronic energy, and he had a frightened look on his face.

Jeremiah was one of Doc's very best inventions—even if he had gotten lost in a Chinese fortune-cookie computer and had his verbal memory chips all scrambled. He was made completely of electrical energy, which meant that he wasn't exactly "alive." But don't try telling that to him. When he wasn't hanging out in Doc's computer, he spent his time in Sean's digital watch, or the handheld computer game Melissa kept in her backpack. Normally, he was fun. But when he got upset or scared, look out!

"No mummies," Jeremiah said, turning a deep shade of purple. "They're bad! They're evil! All those horrible bandages, walking around scaring little kids! I hate 'em!" He looked at Sean's new pants. "I hate 'em even worse than those new pants."

"But, Jeremiah," Melissa began, "mummies don't really

do those things, they're just—"

"I know what they are! I've seen the movies. Brrrrrr!" He went from purple to green to red and back to purple again. "They give me the creeks!"

"That's creeps," Sean corrected him. "And, besides, those are just movies. They're not real."

"Oh yeah? Then you tell me why that mummy's not at the museum. He's probably gone out for a midnight scroll!"

"That's stroll," Sean corrected.

"He's probably out there right now, devouring somebody."

"Devouring somebody?" Melissa asked. "Don't be silly. Someone probably stole him. After all, he was a very rich king, and I'll bet there's a lot of expensive jewelry under all those bandages."

"I'm not listening," Jeremiah said, folding his arms across his chest to show he meant business. "Besides, you know what they say . . ."

"No," Melissa sighed, fearing the worst. "What do they say?"

" 'Early to bed, early to rise, and your girlfriend goes out with some other guy.' "

"What in the world does that have to do with mummies?" she asked.

"How should I know!" And then . . .

Poof!

. . . he disappeared from Sean's watch. Just like that.

Melissa shook her head. "I think he's got a few more circuits loose."

"Probably," Sean agreed, "but he gave me an idea."

"Now what?" Melissa sighed.

"Let's go over to Doc's and see if she can help."

WEDNESDAY, 15:02 PDST

As usual, Doc was in her laboratory, bent over an assortment of gears, electrical wires, and other gizmos scattered across her work table.

Standing silently next to her was a huge metallic robot. Red and blue lights blinked on and off in a control panel on the creature's chest.

Doc looked up and smiled when the kids came in, but then she immediately went back to her work.

What's up, Doc? Sean signed.

Doc almost smiled at the Bugs Bunny joke. Almost. She did, however, sign back to him, *You're getting very good at signing, Sean.*

Sean beamed proudly. Actually, you didn't need to know sign language to talk to Doc. Even though she was deaf and mute, she was an expert at reading lips. Besides, she always kept a portable keyboard and monitor close at hand.

Normally, the two talked by typing messages back and forth. But Sean and Melissa had also been studying hard to learn to sign.

"It's easy to see what she's working on," Melissa said to her brother. "She's making improvements to Domesticus IV."

Doc shook her head and typed: *Not exactly. This is Domesticus V.*

"Domesticus V!" Sean exclaimed. "Wow! I'll bet this guy can really—"

Fly? Doc typed. *Yes, as a matter of fact he can. At two hundred miles an hour, to be exact.*

Wow! Melissa signed. *What else can he do?*

Besides all the normal stuff, you mean? Doc typed. *If my calculations are correct, he can run almost as fast as he can fly, he can dive to a depth of one thousand feet, he can see through walls, and he can speak seventeen languages!*

Melissa shook her head in amazement. "Sounds like Superman," she said.

"Yeah," Sean agreed. "Except he doesn't even have to worry about kryptonite." He picked up a stack of complicated schematic diagrams that had been spread across Doc's workbench. *Man, oh man*, he thought. *She's come a long way from the days of Domesticus I.*

He shook his head remembering what a disappointment Domesticus I had been. For some reason, Doc never could get that bucket of bolts to work right. But comparing that old thing to her new model . . . well, it was like comparing the Wright Brothers' first airplane with the space shuttle. He wondered what had ever happened to Domesticus I. *Probably wound up in some junkyard*, he figured.

His thoughts were suddenly interrupted by his sister's whining voice. "Sean," she said, "please don't get any crazy ideas. Remember what happened with Domesticus IV."

"How could I forget," he whined back. "I'm still paying for it."

Domesticus IV was Doc's "household servant," a robot that was programmed to do things like scrub floors and wash windows. Sean got the bright idea that he and his sister could use Domesticus to get out of their weekly household chores.

But, as usual, Sean's bright idea didn't exactly work out the way he'd planned. Instead of a household servant, Domesticus IV had gone on a rampage that had pretty much destroyed their neighborhood. And, at the moment, Sean was using his allowance to pay back the neighbors for all the damage he'd caused. At the rate of three dollars a week, he figured he'd have the debt paid off by the year 2057.

Over in the corner, Doc's TV was tuned to the afternoon movie, *Godzilla's Great-Grandson Meets the Nephew of King Kong's Brother-in-Law*. Just when it got to the good part (you know, where the giant ape is about to eat the giant thunder lizard for breakfast), the screen went blank. A moment later, an excited voice shouted, "We interrupt this program to bring you a special bulletin from Channel 42 News!"

Suddenly reporter Rafael Ruelas was on the screen. He stood in front of the empty sarcophagus at the museum. "Good afternoon," he said. "I'm coming to you live from the Midvale Museum, where the crime of the century has taken place."

Crime of the century? By Melissa's count, Ruelas had already reported sixteen "crimes of the century" in the last year alone. The guy gave new meaning to the word *overdramatic*. And now, as he continued to rant and rave, Mr. Hakeem Haddad stood beside him, looking very uncomfortable.

"I understand that some brazen thief broke into the museum under cover of darkness and stole the mummy of King Tut-Tut the Thirty-Third." Ruelas thrust his microphone into Mr. Haddad's face. "Is that correct?"

"Well, I don't really—" Haddad began.

Ruelas pulled the microphone back. "And they tell me that this mummy is worth millions and millions of dollars. Would you care to comment?"

"Well, I wouldn't go that far, but—"

Every time Haddad tried to talk, Ruelas pulled the microphone away before he could finish.

"And you believe this is a sinister plot perpetrated by Midvale's enemies?"

"I never said—"

Ruelas grabbed the microphone and spoke back into it. "There you have it, folks." He scowled hard at the camera. "From the mouth of Mr. Hakeem Haddad himself. Un-American forces are at work here. Forces that wish to destroy the very foundation upon which the community of Midvale is built. There can be little doubt that Midvale—and, indeed, the entire American way of life—is under attack!" He smiled. "And now back to our movie."

Melissa shook her head. "How in the world could he get all that out of the mummy's disappearance?" she asked.

"Well, I, for one, believe he's right," said an electronic-sounding voice. Jeremiah was back, this time glaring out at them from Doc's TV. "Have you noticed there are more and more weirdos running around the streets of Midvale these days?" he demanded.

"Define *weirdos*," Sean said.

"You know. Weird people. With strange customs.

Dangerous people. Foreigners."

Melissa began to protest. "But, Jeremiah—"

Jeremiah ignored her and kept talking. "That Haddad guy seems kind of weird to me. I wouldn't be surprised if he had something to do with it."

"But, Jeremiah," Melissa protested, "why would the man steal his own exhibit?"

"Who knows why those people do what they do?" Jeremiah shrugged. "All I know is that I'm proud that I was born in America . . . a country where a poor man like Abraham Washington . . ."

"You mean—"

But Jeremiah was on a roll and would not be interrupted. ". . . a poor man who was born in a log cabin that he built with his own two hands . . ."

"Jeremiah, how can he be born in a cabin that he built—"

". . . can grow up to be president of this great country. And that, gentlemen and ladies, is why I'm proud to be born an American!" Jeremiah finished the last sentence with a grand flourish, bowed, then waited for the deafening applause.

Of course, there was none. Only Sean coughing slightly, clearing his throat, and gently pointing out, "Uh, Jeremiah, you weren't exactly 'born.' "

"I'm afraid Sean's right," Melissa agreed. "And how

many Americans do you know who have green skin, red eyes, and orange hair?"

But before Jeremiah could respond, Doc typed on the screen: *I'm ready to give Domesticus V another test run. Sean, do you want to do the honors?*

"You bet," Sean said. He took the remote control in his hands. "What do I do?" he asked.

It works two ways, Doc typed. *You can do it like I do—by pushing those buttons there at the top—or he'll respond to voice commands. Just talk into that little gray microphone, right there on the remote, and tell him what you want him to do.*

"Really?" Sean asked.

Doc nodded.

Sean glanced at Melissa, who looked anything but happy.

"I think I'll try the buttons first," he said. Then, taking a deep breath, Sean pushed the big red one right in the center.

But nothing happened. Domesticus V just stood there like a rusty suit of armor.

Sean pushed the button again.

Repeat in the nothing department.

He pushed a third time . . . *hard.*

Suddenly the big robot whirred to life. Melissa gasped as Domesticus V turned his head to the left, then to the right. Next, he lifted his hands to his face and examined them. And, finally . . . he began to run!

He ran straight ahead, until . . .

K-BANG!

. . . he knocked over a tray full of tools and parts. Then . . .

K-POW!

. . . he sent a table lamp smashing to the floor. Then . . .

K-RATTLE . . .
K-RATTLE . . .
K-RATTLE . . .

. . . he bounced down the stairs. Until, finally . . .

K-BOOM . . .

. . . he broke through the wall and started down the street . . . just like old times.

"Oh no!" Sean shouted. "We've got to stop him!"

3

What's the Matter, Cat Got Your Voice Chip?

WEDNESDAY, 15:50 PDST

Sean, Melissa, and Doc ran through the gaping hole in Doc's wall, but Domesticus V was already one hundred yards ahead and running at full speed.

"Look out!" Sean shouted. "Don't—"

BLAM!

Too late. The metal monster crashed through the Johnsons' fence.

"Stop!" screamed Melissa. As she chased after the big robot, she noticed the Johnsons' automatic garage door was opening and closing, opening and closing, opening and closing.

SMASSSSSH!

There went the Johnsons' birdbath—the replacement

for the one Domesticus IV had destroyed in his earlier romp through the neighborhood. Next to go was . . .

K-THUNK!

Mr. Johnson's brand-new satellite dish—the one that picked up nine hundred channels. *Had* picked up nine hundred channels. Now it looked like one very large and flattened Frisbee.

Doc had promised that this version of Domesticus wouldn't tear up the neighborhood the way Domesticus IV had—and she was right. It was worse! A lot worse. She kept pushing buttons on the remote control, trying to get him to stop, but it didn't even slow him down. Instead, the robot charged straight through the Johnsons' hedge and out into the street.

Next door to the Johnsons', the Clarks' garage door was also bouncing up and down. The same with the Smiths' across the street.

Sean tried his best to keep up with everyone, but he couldn't run as fast as usual because he kept stepping on the cuffs of his baggy pants.

"Well . . . *huff puff*," he panted. "At least . . . *puff huff* . . . he won't be causing any damage if he stays in the middle of the street."

"Don't be so sure," Melissa shouted. "Domesticus . . . LOOK OUT!"

The robot was headed straight for a Federal Express truck on its way to make a delivery.

SCREECH!
SQUEAL!
SKID!

The big truck swerved all over the street trying to avoid the oncoming robot. But nothing worked. When he swerved to the right, the robot swerved to the right. When he swerved to the left, the robot swerved to the left. Closer and closer they came. Any second, they would hit. Melissa, Sean, and Doc could only cover their eyes until . . .

K-RASH!

When they looked up, they expected to see robot parts scattered all over the street.

They were wrong.

Instead, the truck sat in the street, steam spewing from its crumpled radiator. And Domesticus V? Well, Domesticus V had merely bounced off the truck and kept running. The collision had simply spun him around so he was heading off in another direction.

Melissa had had enough. She just couldn't run anymore. She stopped and stooped over with her hands on her knees, trying to catch her breath. "It's no use," she groaned. "We'll never catch him."

"Come on," Sean urged, "don't be a wimp. We've gotta

keep trying! We've gotta keep—"

SCREECH!

They both looked up the street. To their surprise, Domesticus V had suddenly come to a complete stop. Not only that, but

CLANK! CLANK! CLANK! CLANK!

"What's he doing?" Sean asked.

Melissa peered ahead. "It looks like . . . it looks like he's shaking," she said.

Doc arrived at their side and saw it, too. *He's trembling!* she signed. *I think he's afraid!*

All three watched and, sure enough . . .

CLANK! CLANK! CLANK! CLANK!

. . . the robot was trembling so badly, his arms and legs were clanking together.

"We better go get him!" Sean cried.

All three raced toward the stalled robot, but just before they got there . . .

K-PLUMP!

. . . Domesticus V toppled over on his back. Fainted from fright!

"What do you think scared him so bad?" Sean asked.

"I don't know," Melissa replied nervously. "But whatever it is, I sure don't want to run into it."

Unfortunately, she wouldn't be so lucky. Because, suddenly, the nearby bushes began to shake. Melissa gasped, and all three took a step backward. Whoever or whatever it was had obviously run into those bushes. And now it was coming back out to get them.

"Uh-oh," Sean gulped.

"Here it comes." Melissa shivered.

And then it happened. The bushes finally parted and out strolled a . . . cat!

"Meowwwwww!"

The three could only watch, dumbfounded, as the orange alley cat strolled from the bushes, sniffed at Domesticus V, and then began rubbing against him, purring.

"Is this what Domesticus was so afraid of?" Sean asked. He looked at Doc, who just shrugged.

I'll have to go through the programming, she signed. *But I doubt there's anything in there that would make him afraid of alley cats.*

"Well, it sure did something to him," Sean said.

Doc nodded. *Come on*, she signed. *Help me get him back to the laboratory. Maybe I can figure out what went wrong.*

WEDNESDAY, 16:00 PDST

Mrs. Tubbs paced back and forth across her bedroom floor. Her unkempt hair shot off in about one hundred different directions at once. Her eyes were bloodshot, and her brain was pounding.

The voices had been talking to her all day, and she couldn't get them to stop.

"Be quiet!" she shouted. "Please, just be quiet."

But they wouldn't be quiet.

Instead, they kept on mocking her—teasing her—trying to get her to do things she knew she shouldn't do!

What was it they were saying now? *"We won't make it until you order it?"* What in the world did that mean? What did they want her to order?

When the voices weren't tormenting her with their constant talking, they were singing to her. Well, you couldn't really call it "singing" because there wasn't much of a melody. It was horrible. More like yelling and screaming than music.

She felt like she was going out of her mind.

WEDNESDAY, 16:30 PDST

"But, Dad, we've got more important stuff to do," Sean whined.

"Son, we all have chores around here," he said. "And one of the things I expect you to do is wash the dog. It's been over a month since she's had a bath, and I want you to give her one."

"But, Dad, she's not dirty," Sean protested. "I mean, she smells just fine!" He pulled Slobs close to his face and took a deep whiff.

AGGHH! COUGH! GAG!

It was all the poor guy could do to keep from throwing up. Slobs reeked of rotten banana peels, coffee grounds, and spoiled milk—an obvious sign that she'd been spending too much time in the neighbors' trash cans.

"See," Sean said, trying his best to smile, "she's not dirty at all."

"Which would explain why you're turning green," Dad replied. "Listen, son, when your mother died, we agreed we were all going to do our part to keep the family running smoothly. If you hadn't spent so much time arguing with me, you'd be half finished. Now, get busy."

"But what's Misty—"

"Now!"

Sean recognized the tone in Dad's voice and knew he

meant business. "Yes, sir," he mumbled. He trudged into the garage, then headed to the backyard with a large bucket, a scrub brush, and some doggy shampoo.

Slobs took one look and began to whine. She didn't like getting a bath any more than Sean liked giving her one.

"Sorry, girl," he said as he picked up the garden hose, "but it looks like we're not going to get out of this one."

He managed to get Slobs to hold still and went to work. "Good girl," he said as he worked up a thick lather all over the massive pooch. "As soon as I'm finished, I'll give you a big bowl of dog food."

Suddenly Sean smelled something else. It was terrible. Worse than Slobs. And it was coming from the kitchen. "Oh great," he sighed, remembering it was his sister's night to cook. "Maybe I'll join you. Dog food's gotta taste better than whatever Misty's cooking up."

Slobs began to squirm.

"Hold still, girl," Sean said. "I'm almost finished." He reached for the hose.

"Meowrrrr!"

"Precious!" Sean shouted. "Where did you come from?"

Mrs. Tubbs' fat cat stood atop the Hunters' fence, obviously taunting poor Slobs. He began walking back and forth, doing his best to tease the dog.

50

"Meowrrr!"

And it worked. It was more than Slobs could stand.

"Woof! Woof!"

"Slobs, no!"

But it didn't help. The chase began.

Sean lunged for the dog, but he slipped on the wet grass and fell face first in a soapy puddle.

"Meowwr! Hisssss!"

"Woof! Woof!"

Around the yard they ran, the cat barely out of Slobs' reach as she kept snapping her teeth.

Suddenly the back door to the house opened, and Melissa stepped out. "Sean, dinner's ready!"

Precious saw an opening and took it.

"Meowrr!"

"AUGH!"

The cat leaped for the door, running between Melissa's feet.

Slobs followed right behind.

"SLOBS!"

Too late. The big dog knocked Melissa off balance, causing her to stumble back inside until she hit the counter. Trying to catch her balance, she spun around and accidentally grabbed the bowl of spaghetti she'd just fixed. And when she fell, she managed to drag the whole bowl off the counter and directly on top of her.

51

K-SPLAT

Suddenly the ever tidy and oh-so-neat Melissa Hunter sat in the middle of the kitchen floor, wearing a large bowl of spaghetti atop her head.

Meanwhile, the chase continued—cat and dog in and out of the kitchen, cat and dog into the living room, cat and dog into the den and back into the kitchen. Lamps, plants, and assorted knickknacks toppled and scattered in all directions.

And Sean? He stayed right on their tails, trying to stop them. "Slobs! Precious! Slobs, come here, girl." Unfortunately, wherever he stepped, he left huge, muddy footprints.

Finally, Dad, who had been watering plants in the front yard, came in through the front door.

"Meowrrr!"

Precious raced through the open door like a shot.

"What in the. . . ?"

"Woof! Woof!"

Slobs was next.

And then Sean. "Dad, look out!"

And finally Melissa, who had staggered to her feet and was following right behind.

Dad barely leaped aside in time.

Outside, Precious and Slobs turned left at the corner.

Sean and Melissa followed. Unfortunately, as they rounded the corner, they found themselves heading directly for Spalding, KC, and Bear, who were barreling down the sidewalk on their bicycles.

"Out of our way!" KC screamed. "Get out of our—!"

Too late.

K-RASH! K-BAM! K-TINKLE, TINKLE, TINKLE . . .

Cats, dogs, kids, and bikes flew in all directions. It was quite a sight.

After the usual whining, blaming, and complaining, they began to untangle themselves from one another.

"You guys okay?" Melissa asked as she helped KC with her bicycle.

"Yeah," she answered. "But what were you in such a—" She stopped midsentence and began to laugh.

"What's so funny?"

"What's so funny? Do you always go around with spaghetti in your hair?"

"And, you." Spalding pointed at Sean and began to laugh. "What have you been doing? Making mud pies?"

Brother and sister looked at each other. Melissa's head was still covered with spaghetti, and Sean was covered in dog shampoo and mud.

"It's a long story," Melissa sighed. "You sure you want to hear it?"

"Not at all," KC answered in her gravelly little voice.

"That is correct," Spalding agreed. "We are engaged in more important pursuits at the moment. Isn't that correct, Bear?"

Bear nodded. "Yeah. More important presu . . . persup . . . like he said."

"What sort of pursuit?" Sean asked.

"You guys are supposed to be the detectives," KC croaked. "I figured you'd know all about it."

"All about what?" Melissa asked.

Spalding explained. "Someone . . . or some*thing* has left very unusual footprints in the mud over at the park."

"Strange footprints." Bear nodded.

"And there have been all these mysterious noises at night," KC added.

Bear nodded again. "Mysterious noises."

KC's eyes grew wider as she continued. "And have you ever heard so many dogs howling at the moon?"

"What are you trying to say?" Melissa asked.

"Something extremely unusual is occurring throughout our community," Spalding said. "And that missing mummy is the cause of it all."

"What makes you think that?" Sean asked.

"We heard Rafael Ruelas talking about it on TV," KC said. "And we know that your new neighbor, that Azziz guy, is involved."

Sean couldn't believe his ears. "What? Abdul Azziz is a nice guy."

"Oh yeah?" KC retorted. "Meet us in the bushes outside his house tomorrow night at 8:00, and you'll see how nice he is."

"What are you talking about?"

"Take it from me," said Spalding. "That new neighbor of yours is up to more than you think. A lot more!"

4

Mrs. Tubbs: Street-Fighter

THURSDAY, 14:58 PDST

As soon as school was out the next day, Sean, Melissa, and Slobs hurried over to Doc's house. Not only did they want to see if she had any new ideas on finding the missing mummy, but they were anxious to find out what was happening with Domesticus V.

When they arrived in Doc's attic laboratory, the woman was shaking her head in exasperation over the big robot as she pressed one button after another. Spotting the kids, she moved to one of her keyboards and typed, *I can't figure out what's wrong with him. I've increased broadcast power 100 percent, but he still won't respond. And I have no idea why he was so frightened by that cat.*

She ran her fingers up and down the buttons on the control panel, but Domesticus V remained in the corner, the lights in his chest silently blinking on and off.

Here, Doc signed as she handed Sean the remote control. *Maybe if you talk to him . . .*

Sean shrugged and then spoke clearly into the microphone. "Domesticus," he said, "move your arm."

Nothing.

"Move your leg, Domesticus."

Double nothing.

Sean was becoming exasperated. "Come on, Domesticus. Move! Run!"

The big pile of junk just sat there like a . . . well, like a big pile of junk. Sean grew more angry. He kicked at the robot's foot. "Come on. Don't just stand there. Move your arms. Move your feet. Kick! Punch! Hit! Do *something*!"

THURSDAY, 15:01 PDST

Across town, Mayor Jenkins was making an important presentation at the monthly meeting of the Midvale Garden Club.

"It gives me great pleasure," he said, looking over the top of his horn-rimmed glasses, "to present the Gertrude B. Davis Award. This award is given annually to the person who has grown the largest Petunia in Midvale.

Let's have a big round of applause for this year's winner
. . . Mrs. Hildagard Tubbs!"

As Mrs. Tubbs staggered forward to receive her award,
the members of the Garden Club gasped. On a normal
day, Mrs. Tubbs wasn't exactly what you'd call beautiful.
But today she looked absolutely frightening! She hadn't
bothered to brush her hair. Makeup had been dabbed all
over her face in a haphazard way. And she had the wildest
look in her eyes.

At the front of the auditorium, the mayor held out
Mrs. Tubbs' award, but he looked slightly uncomfortable
as she made her way toward him. Actually, he looked
more than uncomfortable. He looked downright scared.

Meanwhile, the voices continued swirling inside poor
Mrs. Tubbs' head. She knew now it was no use to resist
them. She had to do whatever they told her to do. What
was it they were saying now? Okay!

The mayor held the trophy far out in front of him,
hoping she'd just take it and go back to her seat. But
instead . . .

WHACK!

. . . she kicked him hard in the knee.

"Ow!" His Honor grabbed his leg.

Next she . . .

SMACK!

. . . punched him in the nose, breaking his glasses.

"Somebody get this crazy woman away from me!" he screamed.

But Mrs. Tubbs wasn't exactly finished. Not yet. She began . . .

WHACK! SMASH!

. . . kicking him in the other knee.

In an attempt to protect himself, the mayor grabbed Mrs. Tubbs, and the two of them tumbled to the floor. The thirty or so members of the Garden Club rushed to the stage to try to pull them apart, but that only made things worse. Before they knew it, everyone was rolling around in a big pile. Kicking, hitting, biting, scratching! These sophisticated silver-haired ladies were brawling like a bunch of drunken cowboys in an Old West saloon!

Eventually, sirens screamed outside, brakes screeched, and six large policemen rushed into the room.

It took all six cops to pull Mrs. Tubbs off the mayor and get her out of the building. She kicked and hit at them the whole way, but they finally got her into the back of a police car and drove off toward the Midvale jail.

One of the policemen stayed behind to check on the mayor, who was cowering in a corner. His nose was bleeding, his shirt was torn, and huge chunks of hair seemed to be missing.

"Where is she?" he whimpered. "Keep her away from me."

"She's gone, Mr. Mayor," the officer said. "But what happened?"

"I . . . I . . . don't know. I was giving her the Gertrude B. Davis Award, and she just went crazy! I thought . . ." he began to blubber. "I thought she was going to kill me."

The big cop sat down by the mayor. "There, there," he said soothingly. "We've taken that big, bad lady off to jail. She won't be bothering you anymore."

His Honor dabbed at his bloody nose. "That woman is not very nice," he sniffed.

THURSDAY, 19:45 PDST

"We interrupt this program to bring you a special news bulletin."

Guess whose face suddenly filled the Hunters' TV screen?

If you said Rafael Ruelas, you're right.

"I'm getting so sick of that guy," Sean sighed. "And why does he always have to interrupt my favorite show, *Who Wants to Be a Zillionaire?*"

"Shhh!" Melissa shushed her brother. "Maybe he's got

some important news about the mummy."

"That'll be the day," Sean shot back.

The picture on the TV screen changed. Ruelas was sitting next to two men. One was a big, tall, muscle-bound guy. The other was about half his size. The funny thing was that the big, strong guy looked scared to be on TV. The little guy looked like he wasn't scared of anything.

"There's just been an important development in the case of the missing mummy," Ruelas said, "which I personally uncovered after hours and hours of top-notch investigative reporting."

"Really?" The big guy looked genuinely surprised. "But when we called you just fifteen minutes ago, you said you had no idea—"

Ruelas interrupted, talking loudly so no one could hear the rest of the man's sentence.

"Here with me tonight are Harry Cramden and Tom Norton. Gentlemen, tell us what you do for a living."

"We work for Midvale Museum," Tom answered.

"That's right," Harry agreed. "We're drivers."

"And tell me exactly what happened to you this past Tuesday night."

"Well," Tom began. "We were unloading this big, weird crate from Egypt."

"Yeah," Harry nodded. "Weird. Really weird."

"And we never took our eyes off it for a minute, did we, Harry?"

"No, not for a second, Tom," Harry said. "I mean, why would we do that? You think we'd hear a noise and run off because we were scared or something? That would be silly, don't you think?"

"You sure are right about that, Harry. I mean, it's not like we lost the . . . er . . . mummy or anything like that."

"Nope," Tom shook his head. "Kept our eyes on it the whole time."

Ruelas was getting impatient. "Yes, well, that's enough about what *didn't* happen. Please tell us what *did* take place."

Tom and Harry exchanged worried glances, both urging the other to speak first. Finally, Tom took the lead.

"The mummy came to life and tried to kill us," he said.

"Amazing!" Ruelas cried. "Tell us more!"

"Well," Harry said, "there was this strange guy there. I think he's the mummy's master, and he kept telling the mummy to destroy us!"

"And what did he look like?" Ruelas asked.

Harry shrugged. "He was all wrapped up in bandages, and—"

"Not the mummy," Ruelas said. "The other guy."

"He was really short," Harry said at exactly the same time Tom said, "He was really tall."

63

"Uh," Harry said, trying to explain, "he was really short but tall at the same time. Kind of like, you know, he was a giant . . . but he was also a midget. "

"And what else can you tell us about him?" Ruelas asked.

Again they both spoke at once.

"He was bald," Tom said at the same time Harry said, "He had lots of hair."

Ruelas nodded as if this all made perfect sense.

"Wait a minute," said Tom. "I remember something important. He was dressed really weird. Had a turban on his head."

"A turban? You mean. . . ?"

"That's right," Tom answered. "He was a foreigner."

"Ah," Ruelas sighed. "Now we're getting somewhere!"

"Turn it off," Sean complained. "I've seen enough. Those guys are nuts."

"But why would they make up a story like that?" Melissa asked, obviously a little nervous.

"Who knows? Maybe they were so scared by what happened to them that they can't remember. Or maybe they just wanted to get their names in the news."

"Or maybe . . ." Melissa swallowed hard. "Maybe it's true."

"Don't be ridiculous," Sean scoffed.

"Well, I think we ought to go talk to them anyway,"

Melissa said. "Just to find out what's going on."

Sean shrugged. "Whatever." He glanced at his watch. "Hey, it's almost time to meet Spalding and KC."

THURSDAY, 20:25 PDST

"So where's all the weird stuff that's supposed to happen?" Sean sighed.

"Just wait," KC answered. "You'll see."

"We've been here twenty-five minutes already," Sean said, "and we haven't seen anything."

"Yeah," Melissa chimed in. "And I've got a lot of homework."

Sean, Melissa, and Slobs were hiding behind the bushes across the street from Abdul Azziz's house. KC, Spalding, and Bear were also there. They were all waiting for something, *anything*, strange to happen. But so far, everything had been very, very quiet—except for the sound of Bear's crunching and nibbling. He'd gone through four candy bars, two bags of chips, and a couple of cookies. Now he was completely out of food, and he wasn't taking it very well.

"I'm hungry!" he whined. "How long are we going to be here, anyway."

"Shhh!" Spalding said.

"Well, I'm tired. I wanna go home."

"Bear's right," Sean replied. "We've been out here long enough. I told you Abdul Azziz isn't a crook."

"Look!" KC pointed excitedly.

A black, late-model car was rolling slowly down the street in their direction. When it got within one hundred yards of them, the driver cut the lights and coasted to a stop in front of Abdul's house.

Two men climbed out. The headdresses they wore showed that they were of Middle Eastern descent. They glanced from side to side, then hurried to Abdul's door. When they arrived, they knocked softly and waited.

The door opened halfway, and they quickly entered.

"Here comes another car!" Spalding whispered.

Over the next few minutes, three more cars pulled up, each following the same routine. Altogether, eight mysterious-looking men, many in headdresses, had gone up to Abdul's door, knocked softly, and entered.

"So what do you think of your friend now?" KC smirked.

"This doesn't prove anything," Melissa said.

"Yeah," Sean added. "It's not against the law for him to have a few friends over." But even Sean was wondering why the visitors were all acting so . . . well, so strange.

"Grrrrrrr!"

Suddenly Slobs, who had been sleeping quietly behind Melissa, was on her feet. Her fangs were bared, ears were back, and tail stood straight out. Her attention was focused on something in the bushes just behind them.

"What is it, girl?" Melissa asked. "What do you see?"

"Grrrrrrr!"

"Probably just another cat," Sean called over his shoulder as he tried to get a better look at Abdul's house.

But as Melissa watched, something began moving in the bushes behind her.

Grrrrrrr . . .

"Uh, Sean?" Melissa called. Her voice sounded a little shaky.

"What now?" Sean said impatiently.

"I don't think that's a cat." Her voice sounded even more nervous.

Finally, he turned back to her. "Why not?"

Her hand was raised, her finger was pointing, and she was shaking like a leaf. "Not unless you know any five-feet-tall cats wrapped in bandages."

That's when Sean saw it, too. The mummy was coming straight for them!

5

A Cemetery Stroll

THURSDAY, 20:29 PDST

"Look out!" Sean cried. He leaped back toward Melissa, pushing her to the ground. Instinctively, he fell on top of her to protect her. But instead of coming at them, the mummy staggered past and disappeared down the street.

When Sean was sure it was safe, he rose slowly to his feet and extended a hand to his sister. "You okay?" he asked.

"Yeah . . . I think so," she answered. "But you didn't have to push me so hard."

"Sorry." He looked in the direction the mummy had gone. "Maybe we should try to follow him and see where he's going," he said. And then, louder, to the kids who had been ahead of them, "You guys okay with that?"

There was no answer.

"Spalding?"

Nothing.

"KC?"

Silence.

"Where are you guys?"

"They're not here," Melissa said.

Sean nodded. "Probably already home, hiding under their beds. Come on." He grabbed Melissa's arm. "Let's follow that thing!"

"No way," Melissa answered.

"Why not?"

"In case you didn't notice, that mummy is alive!" she cried.

"Misty, there's no way that thing is real."

She pointed down the road. "You tell *him* that."

"Whatever it is," Sean argued, "it's not supernatural. There are no such things as ghosts. You know that."

"But . . ."

"And if it's not supernatural, then it's something else."

"But . . . but . . ."

"And if it's something else, then we gotta find out what that something else is."

"But . . . but . . . but . . ."

"So stop with the motorboat imitation and come on." Without another word, Sean turned and started off.

Melissa hesitated, gave a heavy sigh, and reluctantly followed.

THURSDAY, 20:33 PDST

The jail psychiatrist tapped his note pad with his pencil as he smiled across the table at Mrs. Tubbs. "How does it make you feel when I say the word *Petunia*?" he asked.

Mrs. Tubbs shrugged. "I feel fine." She tugged at her new clothes. "Except for this stupid jail uniform. You know, with a little tailoring, these wouldn't be half bad. But right now . . . well, they're not exactly what I'd call a fashion statement."

The psychiatrist nodded and continued. "And how about the mayor? Have you always hated people in authority?"

"I like the mayor," she replied. "I voted for him twice."

The psychiatrist let out a frustrated sigh. "Mrs. Tubbs, you broke the man's nose and left bruises all over his body. What would you have done if you *didn't* like him."

Mrs. Tubbs lowered her eyes. "I don't want to talk about it anymore," she whined. "Can I go home now?"

"Tell me about your mother."

"My mother was a fine woman," Mrs. Tubbs said, dabbing at her eyes with a tissue. "Of course, there was that time she beat up that pizza-delivery boy."

"Mm-hmm . . ." The psychiatrist nodded, scribbling furiously on his note pad.

"But then," Mrs. Tubbs went on, "she had a good reason."

"Which was?"

"She ordered pepperoni, and he brought anchovies."

The psychiatrist nodded again. "Now I think we're getting somewhere."

Suddenly Mrs. Tubbs buried her face in her hands and began to sob. "I couldn't help it!" she cried. "They made me do it!"

"Who made you do it?" the psychiatrist asked.

"They did!" Mrs. Tubbs sobbed, pointing at her head. "The voices . . . in here!"

The psychiatrist pulled his chair closer. "Go on," he urged.

"It all started the other night when I went to a cookout. All these weird foreign types were there. I think they were Arabs or something."

"Yes. . . ?"

"One of them was named Abdul. He has something to do with that missing mummy. And I could tell right away that he doesn't like Americans."

The psychiatrist was writing faster than ever.

"He kept flirting with me all night."

She batted her eyes at the psychiatrist. "Of course, I'm

used to men flirting with me, but there was something strange about this guy. And then I broke my tooth, and his friend said he was a dentist and insisted on taking me to his office and . . ."

"Uh-huh." The psychiatrist wrote fast but could still barely keep up.

". . . and it's obvious, isn't it?" she banged her fist on the table. "They put some kind of a curse on me! They wanted me to beat up the mayor because they want to destroy America."

SNAP!

The psychiatrist had pressed down so hard that his pencil broke in two. "And what makes you believe that?" he asked.

"Haven't you been listening to Rafael Ruelas's news reports?" she asked.

"No, I haven't," the psychiatrist said as he fumbled for another pencil.

"All I know is that somebody better warn the president," Mrs. Tubbs said. "He may be next!"

The psychiatrist stood up, crossed the room, and summoned Chief of Police John Robertson on the intercom. "Chief," he said, "you'd better get in here. You need to hear this!"

THURSDAY, 20:35 PDST

"Good girl!" Sean shouted. "Keep going, keep going!"

Sean and Melissa followed Slobs as she trotted in front of them, sniffing the sidewalk, hot on the mummy's trail. But strangely enough, as they headed down the street, garage doors all around them began opening and closing, opening and closing. Yes, sir, if they'd had any doubts before, now they knew something weird was going on in Midvale.

"What's with the garage doors?" Melissa cried.

"I don't know," Sean said. "It's just like what happened when Domesticus was on the loose."

Melissa shook her head. "This is so weird!" Then, spotting something up ahead, she cried, "Look! It's him!"

Far down the street, the mummy staggered along, the loose ends of his bandages flapping in the moonlight.

"He's heading for the cemetery!" Sean shouted. "Come on!"

If Melissa had been scared before, she was downright petrified now. But when they reached the entrance to the cemetery, she was relieved to see the sign that read *Closed to the Public at 6:00 P.M.*

"Oh well." Melissa pointed to the sign, trying her best to sound disappointed. "Looks like we'll have to go home."

"What are you talking about?" Sean asked.

"It's after 6:00. We don't want to get in trouble for going in there when it's closed."

"We can't stop now!" Sean insisted. "Come on!" With that, he followed Slobs through the gate and down the dirt road.

"I was afraid he'd say that," Melissa muttered to herself. Then, with a deep breath and a little prayer for protection, she followed her brother.

To say it was a little spooky in the graveyard was like saying the North Pole could be a little chilly. The crosses and gravestones made eerie shadows in the moonlight. Gargoyles looked out with evil stares on their faces. Even the angel statues, which appeared so friendly in the daylight, seemed sinister and threatening.

Up ahead, they could see the mummy stagger in and out among the gravestones.

"I wonder why he came in here?" Melissa whispered.

"Maybe he's headed to the museum," Sean whispered back. "This is the shortest way back there, you know."

"But what if there's a ghost?" Melissa asked.

"There's no such things as ghosts," Sean reminded her.

"I know that," Melissa said. "But *if* there were such a thing as a ghost—and I know there isn't—but *if* there were, then this would be the perfect place for—"

"Hey, duds. What's down?" a voice suddenly cried, and

Melissa jumped about three feet off the ground.

"It's not a ghost," Sean whispered, "it's Jeremiah."

"I know," she said, trying to hide her embarrassment. "I just felt like doing a little exercising."

Quickly covering his watch, Sean whispered to Jeremiah, "Hold it down a little, will you? We're not supposed to be in here."

"Where are we?" Jeremiah asked, trying to look around.

"The cemetery."

"THE CEMETERY!" the little guy cried.

"Shhh . . ."

"Well, listen, I'd love to stick around, but I think I'm going to make like a tree and molt." And then, just like that, he was gone.

Sean and Melissa exchanged glances and shook their heads. When it came to courage, Jeremiah made the Cowardly Lion appear brave. By the time Sean looked back to the mummy, it, too, had disappeared. Unfortunately, there was another little problem.

"Sean . . ." Melissa whispered.

"I see them."

Up ahead, two light beams were heading in their direction.

"Flashlights," Sean whispered. "The groundskeepers.

They must have heard Jeremiah. We're going to get busted."

"What should we do?" Melissa asked.

"I don't know. We've gotta find a place to hide. There!" He pointed to a large set of creepy-looking gravestones in the darkest part of the cemetery. "Let's hide behind those."

"Sean . . ."

"I don't want to go back there, either, but I sure don't want to go to jail. Come on!"

THURSDAY, 20:40 PDST

"Aren't you happy to see me?"

"Meowrrrrr! Hissssss!"

Precious backed away from his owner. He didn't like the way she was looking at him. Not at all! Something was definitely wrong.

"What's the matter," Mrs. Tubbs said. "Didn't you miss me when I was down at the station with the mean old police?"

Precious cocked his head to one side and tried to look cute (which wasn't easy for an animal a couple hundred pounds overweight). "Meowr?"

"Don't worry, baby. I'm home now."

Precious tried to run, but before he could scramble away, Mrs. Tubbs bent down, grabbed him, and scooped him into her arms.

"What's that?" she said, straightening up and listening as if someone were talking to her. "Yes, yes," she said. "You're right. I am worth it. Even if it does cost more, I am definitely worth it!"

She threw back her head and laughed. A loud, uproarious laugh that made the fur on the back of Precious's neck stand up. She marched to the door, flung it open, and, with Precious still in her grip, headed out into the darkness.

6

A Mummy Makeover

THURSDAY, 20:51 PDST

Melissa peeked around the corner of the gravestone they were hiding behind. The two groundskeepers were so close she could see their eyeglasses glinting in the moonlight.

Sean grabbed her and pulled her back down. "Careful," he whispered. "They'll see you."

The groundskeepers were nearly upon them.

"It was right around here," one of them said.

"And you said it was. . . ?"

"A voice," the first man replied. "I heard someone talking."

Melissa was shaking so badly, she was certain the groundskeepers could hear her knees banging against each other. She closed her eyes tightly and tried to force herself to be calm.

The second man swept his flashlight around the area.

"I don't see anything," he said. "Are you sure you—"

"Meow!"

He began to laugh. "How about that?" he said. "It must be a talking cat. Great, we'll make a fortune on the talk-show circuit."

"But I'm telling you, Ralph, I heard a voice!"

"Here, kitty kitty," the other called. "Nice kitty. Can you talk?"

"Meow!"

"Maybe he doesn't speak English. *Habla Español?*" he asked.

"Meow!"

"No, it looks like he only speaks Cat."

"Knock it off, Ralph," said the first groundskeeper as they turned to head off. "You're not funny."

Their conversation grew fainter as they walked away, but Sean and Melissa stayed put until there were no more voices at all.

Finally, Sean let out a long sigh. "Boy, that was close."

"What do we do now?" Melissa asked.

Sean shrugged. "I guess we give up. The mummy's long gone by now."

"Yeah," Melissa agreed with a sigh of her own. "That's fine with me. Come on, Slobs, let's get out of here."

They'd barely stepped out of the cemetery and started down the road for home when . . .

WAAAAAAAAAAH...

... the shriek of a police car's siren filled the night.

A moment later, the car flew past the kids, its lights flashing brightly.

"You think that has something to do with the mummy?" Melissa asked.

"There's only one way to find out," Sean said. "Let's go!"

They took off running in the direction of the car. Fortunately, they didn't have far to go. It had come to a stop in front of the convenience store on the corner of Elm and Eighth.

Two officers had jumped out and were now confronted by a group of seven to eight very excited, very frightened people. All of them were talking at once.

"One at a time!" the first policeman shouted. "Calm down, now."

"It was a monster!" an old man shouted. "And it nearly ruined my store."

"That's right!" a young woman cried. "I was waiting in line to pay for my Slurpee . . . and it came crashing through that window!"

She pointed, and sure enough, there was a huge man-shaped hole—or was it a *mummy*-shaped hole?—in the store's front window.

"I see." The second policeman pulled his note pad out of his pocket. "And can you describe this . . . uh . . . monster?"

"It was horrible," the store owner began. "It had lots and lots of hair, piled up to here." He held his hand high over his head. "You know, in one of those styles that was popular forty years ago."

"That's right!" the young girl agreed. "And big black circles of mascara under its eyes, and about a dozen different shades of lipstick."

"Lipstick?" the owner cried. "I thought it was blood."

"And the cat," another eyewitness interrupted. "Don't forget the fat cat. What did the thing call it?"

"Precious!" the store owner cried. "It called the cat Precious."

Sean and Melissa exchanged looks.

"So it had a voice?" the first policeman asked.

"Yes," the young woman said. "High, like a woman's. It kept saying something like 'I'm worth it.' "

Sean leaned over to Melissa and whispered, "Are you thinking what I'm thinking?"

She nodded and whispered back. "It doesn't sound like the mummy. It sounds like . . . Mrs. Tubbs."

"Just what did this creature do once it was in the store?" the first policeman asked.

"It stole a bunch of stuff," the store owner said.

"What kind of stuff?"

"A big can of hair spray. Several tubes of lipstick. Some blush, some mascara, and . . ."

The officer stopped writing and looked up from his note pad. "Makeup?" he asked. "The monster stole makeup?"

"Over a hundred dollars' worth," the store owner said. "And only the best kind, too. None of the cheap stuff. I just know it's got something to do with all those weird people in town. All those, you know . . . foreigners Rafael Ruelas keeps talking about!"

Several people in the crowd shouted their agreement.

"This crime wave has to stop!" the owner cried. "And the best way to stop it is to round up all those foreigners and send 'em back to where they came from."

"Those people are trouble!" the young woman agreed.

"They don't belong here!" someone else cried.

"Excuse me, officers," Sean said. "We saw something this evening that—"

The first policeman cut him off. "Can't you see we're busy here, son?"

"I know, but—"

"We're dealing with potential terrorists."

"But we just—"

"Go to the station and file a report. We may be dealing with a matter of national security here."

"But . . . but . . ." Melissa sputtered.

Sean grabbed her by the arm. "It's no use, Misty," he said. "They're too busy to listen. Let's go."

The kids walked silently, lost in thought. How many more crimes would Bloodhounds, Inc. have to solve before the Midvale Police Department took them seriously? They were just a few houses from home when suddenly:

"Look out!"

Three figures charged out of the darkness and narrowly missed them. They wore Halloween masks, but Sean thought he recognized them. "Spalding?" he shouted. "KC?" There was no answer. Nothing but the sound of footsteps echoing on the asphalt as the three "goblins" disappeared into the night.

"What do you suppose they're up to?" Sean asked.

"Who knows?" Melissa shrugged. "And who cares?"

Then they saw it. A message in big black letters spray-painted across the side wall of Abdul Azziz's house:

ARABS GO HOME! WE DON'T WANT YOU HEAR!

Melissa glanced at Sean. "Look at the way they spelled *here*."

They both turned back to the house and then, in perfect unison, said the same name:

"Bear!"

7

Strangerer and Strangerer

SATURDAY, 10:30 PDST

KNOCK! KNOCK! KNOCK!

Sean groaned and pulled the covers up over his head. "Go away! I wanna sleep!"

"Sean!" Melissa called from the other side of the door. "Are you awake?"

"No!" he shouted. "It's Saturday. Leave me alone."

KNOCK! KNOCK! KNOCK!

Angrily, Sean threw back the covers, crawled out of bed, and strode over to yank open the door. "What do you want?" he demanded.

Melissa shrank back in mock horror. "Help! It's the Midvale Monster!"

"Very funny," he mumbled.

"Well, you should see yourself," she laughed. "You really are a mess in the morning. Good thing you aren't out on the streets, or Rafael Ruelas would *really* be upset."

Sean wasn't in the mood for jokes. "This better be important for you to wake me up so early on a Saturday!"

Melissa looked at her watch. "Early? Since when is 10:30 early?"

Sean shook his head. "Would you please tell me what you want?"

"There's been another sighting."

Suddenly Sean was wide awake. "Another one? That makes six in the past three days. What happened this time?" he asked.

"It's on TV right now," Melissa replied.

Quickly, Sean followed Melissa downstairs. He was surprised to see his father in the den reading the newspaper.

"Dad, what are you doing home? Why aren't you down at the radio station?"

Dad shrugged. "I've been spending much too much time down there lately. Besides, Herbie can take care of it."

Sean shook his head. Every time Dad left Herbie in charge, he had to work twice as hard to clean things up when he got back.

Over on the TV, Rafael Ruelas's face was red with anger. His arms flailed wildly as he ranted and raved

86

against all the "monsters" the "foreigners" were bringing into the community.

"It's a miracle that no one has been seriously injured, or even killed, by these horrible creatures!" Ruelas shouted. "If the Midvale police won't do anything about it, it's up to the law-abiding citizens of Midvale to take things into their own hands!"

"Which one was it this time?" Sean asked.

"Which what?" Dad asked.

"Which monster."

"Was it the mummy," Melissa asked, "or that thing that could have been. . . ?"

"Mrs. Tubbs?" Sean finished her sentence.

"Mrs. Tubbs?" Dad chuckled. "I hadn't heard about that. All I know is that something came out of the dark and scared this poor lady half to death."

"Well, if you'll excuse me," Melissa said, "this looks like the same old stuff, and it gives me the creeps. So I'm going to go fix us some breakfast." With that, she headed toward the kitchen.

"Dad," Sean protested, "aren't you going to stop her?"

"Be nice," Dad answered. "I'm sure it'll taste great." Then he whispered, "And even if it doesn't, it won't kill us."

"I heard that!" Melissa called from the kitchen.

Once again, Dad chuckled.

Sean turned to the TV and watched as Ruelas interviewed an elderly woman with blue hair. She held a small, furry creature in her lap. At first, Sean wondered what she was doing holding a rat with a pink ribbon in its hair—until he realized it was a little white poodle.

"I was taking Fifi for a walk last night," the woman said, "when—"

"When a horrible, menacing creature came out of the shadows, growling and snarling?" Ruelas asked.

"Well, no . . . actually, it wasn't like that. It just walked on past me, and—"

"And you were sure you were a goner," Ruelas said. "You were lucky to escape with your life."

"No . . . no . . . I didn't really feel that I was in danger because—"

"Because you were so scared you didn't have time to think!" Ruelas shouted.

"Good grief," Sean yelled at the TV. "Let her tell her own story."

"Well, I think poor Fifi was kind of scared," the woman finally agreed.

The camera cut to an extreme close-up of Ruelas with a smug, self-righteous grin. "There you have it, folks," he said. "Midvale is being stalked by a creature so vile, so evil, that no one is safe. Not even an innocent little doggy like Fifi here."

"GRRRR. . . . YAP!" Innocent little Fifi snapped viciously at Ruelas's arm.

Sean looked on, smiling, until he noticed some movement in the kitchen. Melissa was running back and forth. He couldn't tell for certain, but it looked like her apron might be on fire!

"Misty, you all right?"

"I'm fine, I'm fine!" she shouted. Then he heard the hiss of the fire extinguisher and saw a small cloud of smoke billow out of the kitchen.

"You sure?" Sean got up to help, but Dad, who had his back to the kitchen and couldn't see, motioned for him to sit back down.

"She'll feel better if she does it herself," he said.

"Yes, but—"

"Trust me on this," Dad said.

Reluctantly, Sean sat back down. The smoke was just about gone now, so he gradually returned his attention to the TV.

On screen, Ruelas continued the interview while at the same time shaking his arm, trying his best to get the little dog to let go of it. "Is there anything else you'd like to add, Mrs. Hardenflooper?"

The old lady cleared her throat. "Well, actually, I thought the monster was kind of nice. I'll bet he's a handsome feller underneath all them bandages. If he'd asked me, I probably would have gone out with him. Not that I'm desperate, but I haven't had a date since Mr. Hardenflooper passed away, and that's been over ten years now."

Ruelas swung his arm around and around until little Fifi finally released her grip and went flying through the air.

"YIP! YIP! YIP!"
CRASH!

Mrs. Hardenflooper continued, unfazed. "And if anyone out there is interested, my telephone number is . . ."

Ruelas grabbed the microphone away. "Thank you, ma'am." Then turning back to the camera, he began his wrap-up. "So there you have it, folks—hideous creatures on the loose, thanks to the infiltration of these new foreigners into our beloved city." He smiled. "And now back to our Saturday-morning movie, *Godzilla Versus the Three Stooges.*"

Suddenly Moe was back on screen, giving Godzilla a good poke in the eyes, while Curly looked on, laughing with his trademark "Nyuk! Nyuk! Nyuk!"

Dad aimed the remote and clicked the Off button. "That's enough of that," he said. "That guy's really getting on my nerves."

"But I like Curly," Sean protested.

"I'm talking about Rafael Ruelas," Dad said. "I'm really sick of him always trying to stir up trouble."

"I guess it's good for ratings," Sean said.

"It may be good for ratings, but it's not good for people. Now he's blaming everything on our Arab neighbors here in town. I mean, look what those vandals did to Abdul Azziz's house last night." Dad sighed heavily and shook his head. "When are people going to learn that we're all created in God's image and that He loves us equally?"

Before Sean could respond, the sound of the hand mixer suddenly roared from the kitchen. For the briefest moment, Melissa staggered into the living room, holding a bowl with one hand and the spinning mixer with the other. She was putting up quite a fight, but it looked like the mixer was getting the better of her. You could tell by the way the gooey batter sprayed everywhere. She staggered back into the kitchen as the mixer continued to roar.

"Sis. . . ?" Sean called.

Suddenly there was silence. A moment later, Melissa stuck her head back into the room and smiled sweetly. "It's almost ready. I hope you're hungry."

Sean gave a reluctant half nod, then returned to the subject of Rafael Ruelas. "I know we're supposed to treat everybody equally," he said to Dad, "but we saw some strange people coming in and out of Mr. Azziz's house the other night."

"Strange?" Dad asked.

"Yeah. They were acting funny, and—"

"Son, just because people act differently than we do doesn't make them worse than us. And it certainly doesn't mean they have anything to do with this monster business."

"I know, but—"

Once again, the mixer came to life in the kitchen, followed by Melissa screaming, "Let go of my hair!"

Sean glanced back to the kitchen doorway and saw his sister running back and forth with the beaters twisted into her hair.

"Uh, Dad . . . I really think she needs our help."

Dad nodded and started to rise to his feet. "Maybe you're right."

But by the time they entered the kitchen, Melissa had managed to shut off the mixer and get the food on a platter. What type of food it was, Sean wasn't sure. Pancakes? No, pancakes weren't that thick. Biscuits? Well, biscuits didn't usually smell quite like that. And whatever it was, it had huge clumps of Melissa's hair sticking out of it.

Yum.

"Uh . . . honey," Dad smiled nervously. "Exactly what do we have here?"

"Oatmeal," Melissa said.

"Oatmeal, is it?"

"That's right," she beamed.

"Well, you know, it really looks delicious." Dad tried his best to sound kind. "But is anybody here in the mood for Denny's?"

Suddenly Sean was racing to get his jacket. So was Dad. And, come to think of it, so was Misty. . . .

SATURDAY, 11:45 PDST

After breakfast, Sean, Melissa, and Slobs decided to walk over to the museum to search for clues. They hadn't gone more than a couple of blocks when a voice shouted from behind them, "Hey, what are you kids up to?"

Sean and Melissa spun around to see the angry red faces of a chubby, middle-aged man and his wife.

The woman peered closely at them for a moment—so close that Sean could tell she'd had an onion omelet for breakfast. Finally, she pulled away and turned to her husband.

"It's okay," she said. "They look like fine, upstanding Americans to me."

"Are you sure," he said. "You can't be too careful. They might be Canadians . . . or . . . out-of-staters!" He spit the words out as if they were distasteful.

She looked again, closer. "No. They don't have those beady eyes out-of-staters usually have. I think they're okay."

With that, the couple continued on down the street.

"This is crazy!" Sean said. "What is going on in this town?"

"Nobody trusts anybody who's different from them," Melissa said.

"Hey guys!" a voice shouted.

They spun around to see Jeremiah staring out at them from a big-screen TV in Bramfeld's show window.

"Hi, Jeremiah," Sean said.

"I've just been doing a little brainspraining," he said.

"You mean brain*storm*ing," Melissa corrected.

"Whatever," the little guy said. "But it just dawned on me . . . you people aren't electric!"

Sean and Melissa glanced at each other. "Yeah . . . so . . ."

"So how do I know if I can trust you?"

"Jeremiah?" Melissa sighed. "We're your friends."

"Maybe. But you're not even green!" Jeremiah shouted. "I need to be with my own kind! I need to be with people just like me that I can trust!"

"Jeremiah . . ." Sean started.

But Jeremiah gave him no time to answer. Instead, he clinched his little fist and raised his right arm in a green-power salute. "Electric power to the people!" he shouted. And then . . .

Poof

. . . he was gone.

"Oh brother," Sean groaned. "Even Jeremiah is acting weird."

"You mean *weirder*," Melissa corrected.

SATURDAY, 19:12 PDST

Unfortunately, they could find no further clues at the museum. So, later that evening, Melissa decided to look through some books on ancient Egyptian history she'd checked out of the Midvale Public Library. Who knew? There might be some information in there that would help them find the missing mummy. She picked up her third—or was it fourth—book and began to read:

People had settled on the desert margins of the Nile Valley, but their Neolithic successors descended to Upper Egypt and developed three predynastic cultures . . .

Melissa tried to be interested, but the stuff was boring

95

in a major put-you-to-sleep kind of way. Before she knew it, her eyes grew heavy. Gradually, her head slumped forward until, finally . . .

SNXXXXXXX!!

. . . she began to snore. But only for a moment. Because, almost immediately, Slobs began to bark.

Melissa jerked awake. She heard angry voices shouting in the night. Then there was the unmistakable sound of glass shattering. She jumped up and ran to her window to look out.

It was coming from Abdul Azziz's house!

8

Mummy Mia, Is That You, Mrs. Tubbs?

SATURDAY, 19:50 PDST

When Sean, Melissa, and Slobs arrived at Abdul Azziz's house, their father was already there. He stood on the front porch with Abdul, facing a very angry mob. Someone had tossed a large rock through Abdul's living room window, and some of the men were holding torches, threatening to burn his house down.

"Why are you doing this?" Abdul pleaded. "I have not done anything!"

"We don't want to hear your lies!" yelled a man with a torch. He stepped forward and pointed an angry finger in Abdul's direction. The man was tall and thin, with a thick handlebar mustache and bushy sideburns. It was obvious from the way the others looked at him that he was their leader. He started up the porch toward Abdul.

Immediately, Dad stepped between them, and the man came to a stop. "What are you doing, Thomas?" Dad said to the man. "Abdul hasn't hurt you."

"This isn't your affair, Hunter," Thomas said. "But if you don't stay out of the way, *you'll get hurt.*"

"How can you defend this man when his monsters are tearing up our city?" a woman shouted from the crowd.

Dad turned to her and answered calmly, "Nothing's tearing up our city but this unfounded hatred of yours."

The group stirred angrily.

Dad tried to reason with them. "Look, just because he wasn't born in America doesn't mean—"

"Maybe you're one of them, too," an older man shouted.

Melissa grabbed Sean's elbow. "They're gonna hurt Dad," she whispered. "We gotta do something!"

"Like what?" Sean asked.

Just then a small car came barreling down the road and screeched to a stop right in front of the house. The crowd turned to watch as the driver emerged. He was a young, skinny kid with almost no hair. "I got her, Thomas!" he shouted. "I got the witness!"

"Great," Thomas answered. "Bring her on up here."

Melissa stood on her tiptoes, trying to get a better look. For a second, she thought they were bringing a clown from the car. Then she realized that it wasn't a clown under all that makeup. It was Mrs. Tubbs!

Her hair was piled high, makeup was smeared all over her face, she wore several shades of lipstick, and there were large, dark mascara rings below her eyes.

Melissa's mind spun as she tried to piece it all together. "Sean," she whispered, "are you thinking. . . ?"

"That *was* her at the convenience store," he said. "She fits the description perfectly."

The driver escorted Mrs. Tubbs through the crowd directly toward Abdul.

As she passed the kids, Melissa's mouth fell open.

"Sean!" she whispered. "Did you hear that?"

"Hear what?" he asked.

"The voices coming from . . . Mrs. Tubbs' head!"

"But how could you hear. . . ?"

"I don't know!" she exclaimed. "But I did, and it sounded exactly like . . . like Herbie! Giving the 8:00 news!"

Now Mrs. Tubbs was close enough to see Abdul, and she cried out, "That's one of them! Him and this other guy who claimed to be a dentist. They put a spell on me and caused me to beat up Mayor Jenkins!"

"What?" Abdul asked in astonishment.

"Yes, yes!" Mrs. Tubbs cried. "That's exactly what happened! When that dentist put a filling in my tooth, he also put a spell on me. Ever since then, they've been taunting me. Making me crazy. Telling me to punch the mayor . . . and kick him . . . and punch him again. That's why, at 3:00 Thursday afternoon, I beat the poor man to a pulp."

"Did she say 3:00 Thursday?" Melissa whispered. "Wasn't that when we were over at Doc's?"

Sean nodded. "That's right. And I was using the remote control. But it didn't have any effect on Domesticus."

"Maybe not on Domesticus," Melissa answered. "But do you think. . . ?" She slowly turned to Sean.

Sean looked at her and frowned. "What are you saying? That Mrs. Tubbs heard *my* voice in her head?"

She looked at him, raising an eyebrow. "Well . . . is there any way she could be . . . I don't know . . . picking up radio waves or something?"

Sean frowned harder.

Melissa continued. "She said the voices in her head were telling her to beat up the mayor. And as I recall . . . you were pretty much giving the same type of orders to Domesticus."

Sean thought another moment, then suddenly snapped his fingers. "I just remembered a story I saw on the news a couple of months ago. Yeah . . . at least some of this is starting to make sense now."

Back on the porch, Abdul was pleading, "I did nothing to this woman," he cried. "And I have nothing to hide!"

"Oh yeah?" Thomas stepped forward. "Then why are all them strange people sneaking in and out of your house at night?"

"But they're not—"

"I saw someone hiding in there when you came out!" a woman shouted.

Thomas gave a sly smile. "So . . . if you ain't got nothin' to hide, let us inside to see what they're up to."

"Please," Abdul held out his hands, "just leave us in peace."

But the crowd would not listen. Instead, two or three of the bigger men shoved past Dad and Abdul. And, despite Abdul's protests, they threw open his front door and stormed inside. Thomas was right behind them.

Inside, huddled together in fear, were six of Abdul's friends. Several opened books were scattered on the kitchen table. Thomas swaggered over and picked one of them up. "Look at this!" he shouted to the crowd. "Just look what they're reading. Probably directions on how to make a bomb, or take over the city or . . ." At last he read the title: " 'American History'?" More than a little puzzled, he turned to Abdul. "What are you reading about American history for?"

"We are all studying to become American citizens!" Abdul explained.

One of Abdul's friends held up a small American flag.

"God bless the U.S.A.," he said.

"But why have you been sneaking around at night?" Thomas scowled.

"They haven't been sneaking around," Abdul argued. "They all have jobs. The only time they have to study is at night. And some of them don't want their families to know what they're doing because they want it to be a surprise."

"So much for Arab terrorists," Dad said, taking the book from Thomas's hand.

But the crowd was still angry and still very restless. Until Thomas, who needed to save face, suddenly had a solution. "Well, maybe this Abdul fellow ain't who we thought he was. But what about that Haddad guy over at the museum? He's the one responsible for the mummy getting loose in the first place!"

"Yeah!" someone shouted.

"And none of this crazy stuff happened till then!" another yelled.

"That's right!" a third agreed. "And he's an Arab, too, ain't he!"

"Come on!" Thomas shouted as he stormed out of the house and down the steps. "Let's go get him!"

"Hold it!" Dad called. "You're making the same mis—"

But the mob had already turned and started off toward

the museum, with Thomas and Mrs. Tubbs leading the way.

"Please!" Dad shouted. "Think about what you're doing!"

But it was no use.

Melissa ran up to her father and threw her arms around him. "Dad, I was so scared for you!"

Dad nodded. "But we haven't stopped them yet. We've got to get to the museum."

"Right, Dad," Sean said. "But we'd better go by Doc's house first."

"Doc's?"

Melissa nodded. "That's right. And we've got to hurry."

"Come on, Dad," Sean insisted. "We'll explain it to you on the way!"

9

Where There's Smoke...

SATURDAY, 20:25 PDST

The angry mob wound its way through the streets of town, heading for the Midvale Museum. Along the way, several other people came out of their houses and joined the crowd. By the time they reached the museum's front door, the group had nearly doubled in size.

There to greet them at the top of the museum's steps was a security guard. He was a bit overfed and wore a shirt that was at least a couple of sizes too small, but that didn't prevent him from doing his job. He raised his hands to stop them.

"I'm sorry, folks," he said. "The museum is closed for the evening. Come back tomorrow morning at 10:00, and I'm sure they'll be happy to give you a group discount."

"Group discount?" shouted Thomas. "We don't need no group discount!"

He waved the torch he was holding. "This is our discount."

"Uh, okay," the guard sputtered nervously. "I think, uh . . . I think I'm beginning to see your point. Maybe if you tell me what you want, I can help you."

"We want to see the guy in charge!" Thomas shouted. Other members of the group yelled their agreement.

"That's right! We want to see Haddad!"

"Bring him out!"

"We want him now!"

The security guard shook his head. "I'm sorry, but that would be impossible. Dr. Haddad is at the theater tonight, and—"

Thomas took a step toward the nervous guard. "Then I suggest you call him on his cell phone and get him over here . . . *now.*"

"But—"

"You've got fifteen minutes," Thomas snarled. "Fifteen minutes, or there is going to be trouble."

"Trouble?" the guard gulped. "What kind of trouble?"

Thomas brought the torch closer and said only one word. "Guess . . ."

Dad and Melissa waited in the car with the engine

running while Sean ran into Doc's house.

Melissa looked at her watch and sighed. "What's taking him so long?"

Dad reached over and patted her hand. "He's only been in there a minute, honey. Patience."

"But we don't have time to be patient!"

"Here he comes now."

Sean arrived and scrambled into the backseat. "Okay, Dad!" he cried. "Hit it!"

Dad dropped the car into gear, and they took off.

But they'd barely started before Melissa yelled, "Hold it!"

Dad stomped on the brake, and everyone lurched forward.

"Where's the remote?" she asked. "You know—the thing you went in there to get?"

"Uh . . . oh yeah, right." Sean shrugged. "I'll be back in two seconds," he said as he opened the door and jumped out of the car.

"Oh brother!" sighed Melissa.

Thomas was growing impatient. He turned to Mrs. Tubbs, who stood beside him. "What time is it, pretty lady?"

"The voices say it's 8:38 under partly cloudy skies," she answered.

He turned back to the security guard. "You've got four more minutes," he growled.

"I've called him," the guard protested, "but it takes more than fifteen minutes to get from the Midvale Playhouse to here."

"Now you have three minutes and forty-eight seconds," Thomas replied.

The guard swallowed and nodded. "He'll be here." Then, under his breath, he added, "I hope. . . ."

Hakeem Haddad's wife wore an elegant gown she had bought for this very special occasion—their twenty-fifth wedding anniversary. She'd spent three hours in the beauty salon that very afternoon getting her hair fixed, and she looked great. Unfortunately, at the moment, her mood was anything but great.

"You promised me an evening at the theater," she pouted as she checked her lipstick in the rearview mirror.

Her husband looked at his watch. The security guard had said he'd better be at the museum in fifteen minutes, and it sounded urgent. Why was there so much traffic tonight? He glanced down at the speedometer.

Eight miles an hour! They'd never get there on time. "Hakeem!"

"Huh? Oh, I'm sorry, dear. What were you saying?"

"I said, you promised!"

"I'm sorry, dear," her husband answered. "I'll make it up to you."

"I can't believe we had to leave right at the beginning of the third act. Now I'll never know how it turns out!"

"It was *Cinderella*," he said. "You know how it turns out."

"Maybe there's a surprise ending this time," she snorted. "And whatever the problem is at the museum, why couldn't it wait?"

Haddad sighed. "All I know is that the guard said it was important. Maybe it has something to do with the missing mummy."

"Mummy shmummy," his wife retorted.

Haddad banged on the steering wheel. "This is ridiculous!" he shouted. "What is the holdup?"

His wife saw it first. "Ducks!" she shouted.

"What?" he asked.

"Ducks," she replied, pointing at the intersection. A mother duck was waddling across the street, followed closely by six fuzzy ducklings.

Haddad shook his head. "How did they get so far from the pond?"

"I don't know," his wife answered. "But there's your holdup."

It was true. Traffic was backed up in all directions as drivers waited for the mama duck and her little ones to make their way safely across the street.

"Great!" Dr. Haddad sighed. "The museum's about to be sunk by a bunch of ducks!"

As Dad turned sharply onto Eighth Street, Sean and Melissa told him what they were thinking.

"We're still not sure what's going on with the mummy," Melissa explained. "But we think that somehow Mrs. Tubbs is picking up radio waves in her teeth."

"Radio waves?" Dad exclaimed. "In her what?"

"In her teeth!" Sean exclaimed. "Well, not really in her teeth. More like in her filling."

"Wait a minute," Dad said. "You mean like that lady in Wisconsin? The one I saw on the news?"

"You saw it, too?" Sean asked.

"Yeah," Dad said. "Something about the metal in her filling pulling in a radio station all the way from Chicago."

"And she almost went crazy before she figured out what was going on," Sean finished the story.

Dad nodded. "That's not the first time something like that has happened."

"And it doesn't look like the last," Melissa said.

"But what's that got to do with the mummy?" Dad asked.

"We're not sure," Melissa answered. "I mean, there's no such things as ghosts, right?" She gave a nervous swallow and looked at Dad hopefully.

"That's right, sweetheart, there are no ghosts."

"Even if they come in the form of mummies?"

Dad smiled warmly. "Even if they come in the form of mummies. There has to be a natural explanation to what's going on."

"And until we find it," Sean said, tapping the remote control in his hands, "we can at least calm down the crowd by explaining what happened to Mrs. Tubbs."

"We're almost there!" Melissa shouted as the lights of the museum came into view.

Thomas motioned for Mrs. Tubbs. "Ma'am?" he bowed politely.

"It's 8:50," she said. "And we'll be back with more music right after these messages."

"He's late." Thomas shook his head. "Looks like it's

time to take things into our own hands."

"Please," the guard begged. "He's on his way. Just give him five more minutes."

The leader turned and faced the crowd. "What do you say? Should we give him five more minutes?"

"NO!" they shouted in unison.

He turned back to the security guard. "You heard 'em," he said. "Now, step out of the way. We got ourselves some exhibits to destroy."

"But those exhibits are priceless," the guard protested.

Thomas pushed him aside, and the mob entered the museum.

"There!" Sean shouted. "Park there!"

Dad zipped into a parking space directly in front of the museum's main entrance. Then all, including Slobs, piled out, running as fast as they could up the twenty-four steps to the big front doors.

But just as he reached the top step, Sean's pants—the new ones that were three sizes too big for him—fell down.

One second, they were fine. The next, they were around his ankles, tripping him. As he fell, the remote control flew out of his hands. It spiraled high into the sky, like a Kurt Warner pass. All heads turned and watched as it sailed through the air in what seemed like slow motion.

Sean jumped to his feet, pulled up his pants, and stretched as far as he could, trying to catch the remote as it plummeted back to earth. It fell just out of reach, bounced hard on the steps, then flew over the edge and into the darkness below.

CLUNK!

"Ow!" someone shouted.

"What was that?" Sean turned to Melissa.

"I'm not sure!"

10

Wrapping Up

Sean raced down the steps, taking them three at a time. When he reached the bottom, he saw a man lying off to the side on the sidewalk. In the dark, it was hard to tell if he was dead or just unconscious. It was, however, a little easier to tell about his wife. She was jumping up and down beside him, flapping her arms like a berserk chicken and screaming, "They shot my husband! Help! They shot my husband!"

Dad joined Sean, and the two knelt down beside the figure on the ground. "It's Hakeem Haddad!" Dad exclaimed.

"The remote control must have hit him on the head," Sean said.

"He's been shot!" Mrs. Haddad kept jumping up and down and screaming, "Help! They shot my husband!"

Dad rose and tried his best to calm her. "Nobody's shot

your husband," he said. "My son hit him with a remote-control device."

"Help!" she screamed again. "My husband has been hit with a—" She suddenly stopped in mid-scream and turned to Sean. "Why would you hit poor Hakeem with a remote-control device?"

"It was an accident," Sean explained. "I'm really sorry. You see, I tripped because my pants were down around my ankles, and—"

"Oh no, a gang member!" she cried. Instantly, she pulled a bottle of pepper spray from her purse and aimed it at Sean's face.

"No, ma'am," he shouted and started for her. Luckily, his pants again fell and again he tripped . . . which meant the eye-stinging spray shot over his head and directly down onto her husband's unconscious face.

Well, he *had* been unconscious. Now he was sitting up, coughing and sputtering. "Where am I? What's going on? Where am I?"

Inside the museum, the mob had made its way to the Egyptian exhibit.

The security guard was still trying to stop them.

"Please!" he shouted. "Don't do anything you're going to regret."

Thomas laughed. "Regret? We're just going to destroy all this evil stuff so Midvale will be safe. And after that, we're going to get rid of all the weirdos who are ruining this town."

The mob cheered its approval.

"I know you're just doing your job," he said to the guard, "but you'd better get out of the way before you get hurt."

Dr. Hakeem Haddad was okay. Except, of course, for the huge bump on the top of his head and the burning in his throat and eyes from his wife's pepper spray.

With Dad's help, he staggered to his feet. "Will somebody please tell me what's going on?" he asked.

"A bunch of people are trying to destroy the museum," Melissa explained, "and we've got to stop them!"

"Only we need the remote control to do it," Sean said. He gestured toward the thick bushes beside them, the ones that lined the front of the museum. "It must have bounced in there. We'll never find it!"

"What are we going to do?" Melissa asked desperately.

"I don't know!" Sean cried.

"Woof! Woof!" Suddenly Slobs came running out of the bushes. And there, gently clenched in her mouth, was the remote control.

"Good girl!" Melissa shouted as she took it from the dog's mouth.

"Way to go, Slobs!" Dad exclaimed.

"Is it . . . broken?" Sean asked.

"No," Melissa answered. "It looks fine. Except for this little dent." She handed it to her brother. "And, of course, all the drool on it."

Sean was the first to reach the Egyptian exhibit, followed by Slobs, Melissa, Mr. Hunter, and Dr. Haddad. Mrs. Haddad was a little farther behind (running in three-inch heels tends to slow a person down).

"Stop!" Sean shouted to the mob. "Mrs. Tubbs isn't under a spell!"

Thomas turned and pointed angrily. "You kids better get out of here if you know what's good for you. Nobody's gonna stop us! Especially no foreigner-lovers like you and your old man."

"Mrs. Tubbs," Melissa yelled, "can you hear me?"

Mrs. Tubbs nodded in reply. "Fifty-two degrees in

Baltimore," she said, "with a fifty percent chance of rain tomorrow."

"She's picking up the evening weather report!" Melissa exclaimed.

"Mrs. Tubbs," Sean said, "we think you're picking up radio waves through the new filling in your tooth. It's just something that happens once about every three billion fillings. . . . not part of a plot to destroy Midvale!"

"You're crazy!" Thomas yelled. "And for the last time, you'd better get out of here if you know what's good for you!"

Sean clicked a button on the remote control and said in a calm, clear voice, "Mrs. Tubbs . . . raise your right hand!"

Mrs. Tubbs' hand shot into the air.

"Now raise your left hand!"

She quickly obeyed.

"Do you hear me, Mrs. Tubbs? Is my voice inside your head now?"

She nodded, and the woman standing next to her stepped back and clasped her hand over her mouth. "I . . . I . . . can hear your voice," she said. "Only it's coming out of her head!"

"It's because this voice-activated remote control uses radio waves," Sean said. "And right now, because we're so close, we're drowning out all the other signals."

"Don't listen to them!" Thomas shouted as he moved toward them menacingly. "They're in cahoots with all those creepy foreigners."

"No, really," Sean explained. "This is just a remote control one of our friends built for her robot. You see, it's either voice activated, or you can push these buttons here."

Some people in the mob were listening, but most weren't. They still seemed eager to do whatever Thomas wanted.

Melissa grabbed the remote from Sean. "My brother's telling you the truth," she shouted. "But see . . . these buttons don't seem to work." She began pushing the buttons rapidly. "See . . . I'm pushing them as fast as I can . . . and nothing's happening. But when you speak into—"

Suddenly, there was a loud . . .

KEE-RASH!

. . . as the mummy exploded through the wall!

The mob screamed and went crazy. "It's attacking!" they cried. "It's attacking!" They began stumbling and bumping into one another. "Run for your lives! Run for your lives!"

And run they did. Eventually the entire group turned around and began running for all they were worth—all the time screaming and shouting. It took less than a minute for them to rush down the hall, tumble down the steps, and run out into the street. It took less than two minutes for their hysterical screaming to fade as they raced into the night.

But Sean and Dad weren't running. Neither was Melissa . . . although she seemed to be spending a lot of time reciting "There are no ghosts, there are no ghosts, there are no ghosts. . . ."

All this as the mummy continued to approach.

"There are no ghosts, there are no ghosts. . . ." Melissa was trembling so hard that she gripped the remote control with all of her might just to stop her hands from shaking.

The mummy stretched out its arms toward them. It was five feet away.

"There are no ghosts, there are no ghosts. . . ." As she clutched the remote, Melissa managed to squeeze all of its buttons, including the big red one labeled *Stop*.

Instantly, the mummy came to a stop, so quickly that its head dropped forward. That's when something *really* strange happened.

As the head dropped forward, the bandages that were wrapped around it unwound and tumbled to the floor.

And there, under all the bandages, appeared the unmistakable, shiny, metallic head of . . . Domesticus I!

SUNDAY, 17:14 PDST

On television, Rafael Ruelas angrily thrust his microphone into the face of Harry Cramden, the museum's delivery-truck driver.

"So why don't you tell us what really happened that night?" he demanded.

Harry looked down and wiped a tear from his eye.

"We're really sorry," Tom Norton, his partner, said. "We didn't mean to cause all this trouble."

"Please continue."

"Well, you see," Harry explained, "we heard this noise, and we ran off."

"It was really scary," Tom added.

Harry continued. "And I guess somehow the crate with the mummy fell into the street. And when we came back . . . when we came back . . ." His voice grew so thick with emotion that he couldn't go on.

Tom patted his partner on the back and continued the story. "When we came back, we saw the whole thing being loaded into a garbage truck."

"We tried to get him back," Harry said. "We really did. But it was too late. When we caught up with that truck and looked inside, old Tut-Tut was smashed flatter than a pancake."

"The sarcophagus was still in pretty good shape,

though," Tom said. "So we dragged it out."

"And while we were in the back of the truck with all the garbage, we saw this metal dummy. . . ."

"So we thought maybe we'd wrap it up in bandages, put it in the sarcophagus, and nobody would ever know the difference."

"We figured the dummy was just a piece of junk that nobody wanted," Harry explained. "We didn't know it was a robot . . . or that it was going to come to life or anything."

Tom nodded.

Harry wiped another tear from his eye. "And I'd like to apologize to all the fine upstanding members of Midvale's Arab community. We are truly sorry we tried to put the blame on you."

Rafael Ruelas grinned like a Cheshire cat as the camera moved in for his close-up. "As you know," he said with as much sincerity as he could muster, "I've been saying for days that there had to be a logical explanation behind this city's apparent encounter with one of the walking dead. Yes, there were those who tried to put the blame on others simply because they were different. But, as I've said all along, such an attitude is wrong and—"

Sean reached up and clicked off the television. "That guy is really something else," he said, shaking his head.

"He sure is," Dad agreed. "But I still don't understand

what made Domesticus I suddenly start working after all this time."

"It was the mummy's cloth they wrapped him in," Melissa explained. "Apparently, it had gold threads in it."

"And?" Dad asked.

"And that completed the electrical circuit, allowing Domesticus I to start picking up signals from the remote control."

"Amazing," Dad said, shaking his head in wonder. "I hope you two know how proud I am of you."

"Because we solved the mystery?" Melissa asked as she plopped down beside him on the sofa.

"Yes, I'm proud of that," he said. "But I'm also proud that you realize being different doesn't make you bad. I'm proud that just because Abdul Azziz is from a different country and a different culture, you didn't see him as being strange or dangerous."

"Well," Melissa said, reaching over to give Dad a kiss on the cheek. "You're the one who taught us that we're all created in God's image."

Dad pulled her closer. "Then I'm proud your Dad is such a great teacher!" he chuckled. "Hey, how's the big guy doing in there?"

Sean laughed. "Since Doc switched to a different frequency, he's doing just fine." He picked up the remote control, pushed a button, and Domesticus V entered the room carrying a plate of fresh-from-the-oven cookies. "Doesn't even make garage doors open and close anymore," Sean said.

"Would . . . you . . . like . . . a . . . snack . . . sir?" Domesticus V held out the tray of cookies to Sean.

"Thank you, Domesticus," Sean said as he grabbed a handful of cookies. "Mmmm! Chocolate chip. My favorite."

"There's still one thing I don't get," Melissa said as Domesticus V offered her a cookie. "Why was he so afraid of that cat?"

Sean shrugged. "Doc was never able to figure that out. At least not yet. Maybe later. But she doesn't think it will ever happen again."

Suddenly a furry orange cat jumped up on the outside windowsill and meowed loudly.

And, just as suddenly . . .

K-LATTER!

. . . the plate of cookies fell to the floor. This was immediately followed by Domesticus V . . .

EEEAAAGGGGH!

. . . shrieking in terror. Then he turned around and took off running right through the . . .

K-RASH!

. . . living-room wall.

"Oh no!" Sean and Melissa cried in unison. "Here we go again!"

By Bill Myers

Children's Series:
Bloodhounds, Inc. — mystery/comedy
McGee and Me! — book and video
The Incredible Worlds of Wally McDoogle — comedy

Teen Series:
Forbidden Doors

Adult Novels:
Blood of Heaven
Threshold
Fire of Heaven

Nonfiction:
Christ B.C.
The Dark Side of the Supernatural
Hot Topics, Tough Questions
Faith Encounter

Picture Books:
Baseball for Breakfast